To, Yvonne !

Enjoy !

Hasan Thebis

Books by the same author

The Fatal Flaw (1987) Published by, Arthur
H. Stockwell Ltd. Devon, U.K.

Journey To Life (2015) Published by, Wesbrook
Bay Books, Vancouver, Canada.

The Medallion (2017) Published by,
AuthorHouse, Bloomington, IN, USA.

THE RESCUE

H.P. KABIR

authorHOUSE

AuthorHouse™
1663 Liberty Drive
Bloomington, IN 47403
www.authorhouse.com
Phone: 1 (800) 839-8640

Published by AuthorHouse 11/13/2017

ISBN: 978-1-5462-1468-7 (sc)
ISBN: 978-1-5462-1466-3 (hc)
ISBN: 978-1-5462-1467-0 (e)

Library of Congress Control Number: 2017916517

Print information available on the last page.

CONTENTS

Dedicated to
The love of my life
My wife
Rasheda

INTRODUCTION

The Medallion, a prequel to *The Rescue,* a science fiction novel by the same author.

In The Medallion, a rouge plant happened to come to the vicinity of the sun and placed it in the solar system, but before it did, some managed to land on Earth and made it their home. For some time they were not aware of their world's predicament. It all began fifteen thousand years ago.

A medallion was given to a trusted person by the aliens, which was misplaced. When found many years later it led to an adventure that triggered the world's disbelief in the message it contained.

Disappointed with the reception it received, the aliens decided to leave Earth and go back to their planet which was comfortably placed in the solar system.

Ten years later, in the '*The Rescue',* Earth was threatened by an asteroid that would have wiped out all life. Was spotted by the aliens and destroyed.

They decided to visit and tell the world. They were surprised to find an alien adversary whom they had banished years before, had returned, had an unchallenged rheostat on robbing gold, and hypnotically controlled the populace. They were forcibly removed and subsequently their world was eradicated.

The visiting aliens helped to restore order in the chaotic world, and meant well to introduce a New World Order to bring peace and harmony. It was not received favorably; but with some persuasion, made an offer they could not refuse!

CHAPTER 1

Under a colossal astronomical dome Dr. Frank Osborne remained pinned to the binocular telescope scanning an area in the Kuiper belt almost holding his breath, then suddenly he dislodged himself, ran to a panel of instruments and sprinted back again to the telescope. He repeated that marathon several times.

His two colleagues working on a bench at the far end just looked at him and wondered what their colleague was up to. They however, continued at what they were doing. Seconds later they were startled by Dr. Frank's loud cry that shattered their serenity, "No, No, Nooo…" he kept repeating.

They were petrified and both stood perplexed as he approached them with his hands waving. "It is coming, history is going to repeat itself, an asteroid a little bigger than the Martian moon Deimos is heading for us."

"What are you saying, are you sure?" Dr. Walker Smith interjected.

"I must have a look, would you like to accompany me Dr. Maki." Both headed for the telescope.

After minutes of scrutinising the two walked out to an adjacent room where Dr. Frank sat in silence.

"Let us double check with Dr. Rochelle, ask her to scan, using her telescope." Dr. Maki Sen suggested.

An hour later she confirmed the approaching asteroid and nick named it 'Inferno.'

"An appropriate name for the time being," Dr. Walker said softly.

"We have to inform headquarters and let them deal with the situation," Dr. Frank suggested.

"Let us not be hasty, spend a few more hours studying its behaviour, and once we have all the information we can make the announcement to the Boss at EW5 Headquarters," Maki suggested.
"Good idea, you both do your homework if it takes you the whole night, and tomorrow we meet and call the Boss. Keep it to yourselves, we don't want panic here." Dr. Frank said and sat morosely thinking.

At seven in the morning Dr. Maki walked in and found Dr. Frank slummed on a desk fast asleep.

Over a cup of coffee he murmured, "It is coming at us in about three and half years."

Dr. Rochelle Wright, in charge of the second observatory on the island's northern tip, drove to meet them, and found the three astronomers sitting in silence, thinking.

"From the present data I have charted a temporary trajectory and its rendezvous with Earth. Will be more accurate once it comes near Pluto. In any case, I am ready to pass the news to London. Do we agree?" Dr. Frank looked at his colleagues one by one. They all nodded their heads, "Go ahead Frank, let's not waste any time," Dr. Rochelle said.

All four sat at a round table with a red coloured phone laying in the middle. Dr. Frank punched a number and waited a few seconds then entered another two digits.

All could hear the ringing tone as it was on the loud speaker. A voice answered softly, "Hello Dr. Frank, It better be good to wake me up, you know it is Sunday and eight in the morning."

"Yes boss but it is most urgent." Dr. Frank said politely.

"I have bad news, we have a state of alert for Earth." He explained the entire situation and waited for an answer.

There was pin drop silence at the other end. His answer was brief, "I will fly over to Twin Peaks Island and be with you by the day after, we will talk then, and by the way stop calling me boss. You may call me by my first name."

"Yes Mr. Justin."

"And no Mr. please, just Justin." He hung up.

Two days later Justin Bloomberg accompanied by his five colleagues, each representing the countries of the EW5 members, arrived at Twin Peak Island. After studying all available data about the approaching asteroid, Justin suggested that the situation should be kept strictly to the senior four at Twin Peak and the EW5 members from London.

It was agreed. "Any announcement to the world would create havoc, social upheaval and chaos. The inevitable will happen, let the people live their remaining days in harmony. Not even heads of governments were to know." That was their decision.

Back in London Justin kept in touch with Dr. Frank on daily basis. Inferno kept coming. Fearing some observatory in the world would soon discover the approaching asteroid, Justin prepared a news bulletin to falsify such reports, and that the asteroid is no danger to Earth, it will be caught by Jupiter's gravitational pull. The news item was sealed and put in a safe. No one else was told about the repot. As time went by there were no mention or even a hint in any newspaper to the relief of Justin.

CHAPTER 2

Twin Peak Island is situated just about twenty miles off the south east coast of South Africa, practically unknown to the outside world except for a handful of highly specialised personnel from Great Britain, Canada, the United States of America, Australia and Japan, which comprise the Earth Watch Five nations, with Justin as its head. Its closest neighbour to the south is Prince Edward Island. The Island is simply called Twin Peak Island, because of its twin peaks, one in the centre rising to 3000 feet and the other to its northern tip just about 2000 feet. The island is five miles wide and fifteen miles long. Population of fifty seven people mostly highly skilled scientists, astronomers, astrophysicists, mathematicians and general staff that control its security.

The Twin Peaks are actually flat plateaus rising above the topographical structure of the land mass hence got its name. On each, there are observatories, large radio telescopes, video and magnetic tape display and analysis system, computer and recording devises, receivers and amplifiers. All funded by the five nations and only they knew of its existence and the work that goes inside. Their world headquarters is in London.

Their main function is to keep a watch on all activities of satellites and outer space. The personnel live a very solitary, restricted outdoor recreational activity under the watchful eyes of the security staff.

Few buildings house the staff and their recreational facilities. The western coastline enjoys a large stretch of sandy beach, further inland a varied vegetation from bushes to high trees cover the entire western mountain slopes of the island. Camouflaged within that growth, an electronic fence surrounds the entire island that can stun an uninvited visitor or animal. A few seasonal streams meander gently emptying into the ocean. The eastern coast forms the mountain spine, with a wall of precipitous drop of varying heights, straight into the ocean, littered with boulders and rocks that go out a few hundred feet. A natural barrier that discourages any trespassers.

Except for the towering astronomical domes the island gives an uninviting appearance to onlookers or uninvited guests. A couple of casual looking boats circle the island keeping a watchful eye on its security.

For the residents, their solitary life is compensated by a life style of a five star hotel, from entertainment to sporting facilities. Thanks to the EW5 catering services.

The island traditionally was known as Demon Island by local tribesmen of South Africa. It earned its name centuries ago when some adventurers tried to settle there but had to leave in a hurry in a couple of days and return with tales that the island was haunted and inhabited by demons that howl and moan all day and night. Many years later in the early twentieth century a British explorer and a seasoned sea captain took the challenge to visit the island. "I will bring you the heads of those demons," he told the tribesmen as he and a team of five crew embarked on their journey.

They first sailed around the island studying its coastline. They anchored near the south western tip and set up their camp on the sandy beach close to the shoreline. Late that night they were awakened by a ferocious whirling sound like someone in agony or pain. It died out as quickly as it had come, then it came back with more violent tones, followed by ghastly howls and suddenly died out with a whimper. They scouted the area for any wild animal that might be prowling nearby. The full moon shown bright, exposed hundreds of feet of clear vision. They found no prowlers of any kind, but an element of fear griped them. Huddled together they slept, but were awakened several times by the repetitious howls and groans that filled the tranquil air. It continued in phases, sometimes soft but mostly violent.

The next day the terrified crew gathered and approached the captain, they wanted to leave the island. Disappointed with their attitude, the captain had to think fast.

"Gentlemen, demons and spirits are old women's tales, there are no such things, it is possible there are wild animals, you are seasoned sailors and have faced many challenges and won. We have weapons and can outsmart any animal big or small. Screw up your courage and let us work as a team to prove to the people back home that they were wrong. A few heads of the wild beasts will solve the myth of demons."

The crew walked away and paced the shoreline, and made a decision. They came up to the captain, proudly one of them said, "Thank you sir captain, for thinking so highly of us, we fought many battles with you, fighting any beast won't be as hard as those wars. We are ready to face the dammed beasts or demons."

7

"Thank you lads, now let us sit and listen carefully where from the sounds are coming. I spent the night concentrating on the direction of those howls and the hissings, and they were coming only from one side of the island. So let us move on to that spot. That would be more likely the abode of whatever it is."

Carefully in a military formation they scanned the terrain to their right and left until they came to the edge of an escarpment where the ferocious howls were deafening. Someone pointed to a small opening on the face of the cliff just about fifty feet up. "That is where the sound is coming from," Someone pointed out. "Those wild beasts must be living in that cave. There may be several of them."

"We are going up there to meet the challenge, beast or no beast, just keep your weapons ready, but no one to use them unless I say so," the captain instructed.

Nervously they exchanged glances, but followed their captain who led the way.

The ground was sandy and moist, their feet sank inches into it, and at the same time they had to hack their way through unruly bushes with prickly long leaves. Further inwards, to their relief the ground became firmer. Steeped gently, with high trees rising up to fifty feet in length. Their upper braches intermingled and formed a canopy. The ground became steeper. They rested for a while, and began the arduous journey to scale up the almost vertical side of the cliff leading up to the orifice, where from the wailing continued as if to warn them not to come any closer.

Projecting rock formations eased their climb, but was painstaking. Using hands and feet, inched their way up, the captain was the first to reach the howling gap. With hands and feet firmly anchored to the side of the cliff, he placed his chin on the tip of the floor of the cave and looked inside. A strong blast of wind almost blinded him, blew his hat and sent it flying, muffled his hair and he almost lost balance but managed to scuffle to the top. His crew watched in terror, frozen to where they held firmly. The captain anchored himself against a jutting rock on the side of the cave, lowered a rope and one by one pulled them up. They bunched together with eyes and ears on the alert, uncertain to what might suddenly leap out at them from within. The captain took the lead and asked them to file behind him with their weapons pointing forward as on a battle field. They moved cautiously, the wind was overwhelming and the yowls were unwelcoming.

The captain moved on stealthily, they followed, and readied for an unexpected ambush, a demon or a monster who might suddenly pounce on them. As they advanced into the cave, it became darker, with twists and turns, filled with scattered chunks of rocks and large dried tree branches, which obstructed the passage. Carefully they maneuvered, at one point there was a sudden gust accompanied by an uncanny whimper and a faint moan. They froze and held their weapons in readiness. They moved cautiously with their guns brandished high. It was getting darker and they inched their way nervously inwards. The captain shouted, "Come on brave lads, nothing to be afraid of, if there was a monster it would have devoured us by now. Just follow me, to make it easy for you, with one hand hold each other by the shoulder and feel the side of the cave with the other. as you move along. One of you hold mine." In a single file they moved on."

Deep inside they got disoriented, when a strong blast of wind almost threw them off balance, but managed to press on in disarray. The howls, wails and shrieks continued fiercely, which further perturbed their concentration. Like blind men they moved on. The passage narrowed, both sides of the cave were brushing against them. Sharp edges of rock tattered their hands.

The captain stopped, he hit a wall, a dead end, but felt a strong torrent of gust from below. Bent down and with his hands sized the opening, sufficient to crawl through. The ghastly strong wind shrieked as his body battled forward. On the other side he stood up, half dazed and shaken. He shouted, "I feels better on this side, crawl through."

The crew heard him but ignored his call. They slid against the wall and barely managed to sit, frightened and disoriented by the continuous eerie hisses that filled the narrow enclosure. The captain shouted again, "What is keeping you, hurry up." His call went on deaf ears.

He waited patiently, then someone yelled, "Go ahead captain, need to rest, we will follow shortly."

"Damn you John for convincing us to go along with the captain," One of them cursed.

"I am sure there is a monster waiting for us, hiding in a hole somewhere. Perhaps on the other side." Another commented.

"Let the captain go on, if we don't hear his scream, it means the coast is clear." Someone put in.

The captain lost his patience waiting, "When you all make up your minds, come through, I am moving on, will wait at the end wherever it takes me," he yelled.

Darkness was overpowering. Moving on, razor sharp edges of rocks bruised his hands, and slowed him down. A sudden gust threw him off balance and he fell, rolled back and his head hit a rock. The captain struggled up, and continued.

Meanwhile, the crew sat thronged together near the small opening, terrified.

"Did you hear a scream?" Someone asked.

"No, only the monster's howls."

"It must be nearby, sorry for the captain. After him it will have us for its dessert."

The captain continued unperturbed. At one point, the path led him to a right angle turn, as he did, spotted a gleam of light in the far distance. Raced up to it and entered a large hollowed section, with a rounded roof top, to his joy, an opening of about ten feet wide, through which he could see the blue sky and the ocean below. He walked to the edge, looked at the waves beating mercilessly at the countless boulders that littered the coastline. The wind was strong and unruly. He looked up at the rounded ceiling, "The wind over the years must have hollowed it, and carved the labyrinth of this cave." He pondered. He let out a smile and shook his head. "How stupid we are?" He said to himself. Suddenly remembered his crew, and let out a mischievous smile, went back a few feet into the cave and fired his gun several times and called out loud, "Come you lazy bones, I have got the beast." He repeated several times and rested behind a rock and waited.

The captain guessed that part of the island must be the narrowest and he was facing east. It dawn on him that all that fuss about monsters and demons came from the wind blowing through the intricate passage of the tunnel. "Fear comes out of the unknown. When one cannot find an answer, invents one, to suit the situation which no one can challenge. That is how we make up superstitions and fantasies." He mused and decided to play a prank on his crew.

"Can you hear me, you old sea salt," he shouted louder, his voice echoed throughout the maze. He waited patiently as they lumbered in. Stood and looked around for their captain. From behind the rock he brandished both hand and said with a gallant voice, "I have the head of the monster."

"Can't see anything but a pair of empty hands," one of the crew said suspiciously.

"In my hands, you fools," the captain muttered and stood up.

"Your hands are empty," another said.

"Sit down and relax you fools. There is nothing on this island, perhaps not even a bird, not to speak of wild beasts and demons. It is all in the wind, go near the opening and experience the strength of it, when it enters this cavity with a force, it is so powerful that it blows through the intricate tunnel, embraces obstacles, and little openings with twists and turns, creates those monstrous reverberation which sound horrendous.

"The principal is the same as in a wind musical instrument, you blow though it and produces sound, and it is as simple as that."

When they told their story back home, it became a topic of conversation in saloons, barber shops and after dinner chats.

But to the superstitious locals and tribesmen it was still Demon Island and nobody wants to go there.

It was for that reason the selection of Demon Island, renamed Twin Peaks Island was an ideal choice to set up all the astronomical facilities without anyone disturbing their peace, as no one wanted to visit it.

CHAPTER 3

Dr. Frank spent most of his time following the progress of the Inferno asteroid. Dr. Maki and Dr. Walker were always at his side.

"Two months had passed, and it continues to proceed. I just hope it gets caught by the gravitational pull of Jupiter, the space vacuum cleaner as we call it when anything comes near its vicinity. If that does not happen, there is one more dangerous possibility, should it enters the Asteroid Belt, may cause havoc by sending hundreds of meteorites to Mars, the moon and the Earth. We will then have hundreds of infernos bombarding us," Dr. Frank came out with a skeptical view.

Dr. Maki was not amused, "I want to hear something more cheerful, how about praying for a miracle."

"Our only hope is Jupiter's gravitational pull, but most likely it is too far to get caught," Dr. Frank said and returned to the telescope.

The inferno's progress has remained unchanged. The four cosmologists at Twin Island collected data from their radio telescopes and kept London informed on daily bases.

Another five months had passed and none of the observatories worldwide had reported or even hinted at the approaching doom's day threat.

Suddenly one day all hopes were shattered to keeping the asteroid a secret. An observatory in Chile saw it coming, after consulting with other observatories worldwide, they announced the tragic news. Newspaper headlines boldly printed, 'Doom's Day Soon', 'Judgement Day in about three years' and 'Next Extinction Soon'.

Dr. Frank called Justin in London.

"Not again, you seem to make it a habit to call on Sundays, what is it this time?"

He explained the situation.

"What, very irresponsible of them, leave it to me to put out a contradictory bulletin, otherwise there will certainly be chaos and upheaval throughout the world." Justin exclaimed. He thought of the bulletin he had prepared, but dismissed it as not sufficient to qualify, he had to come with a more positive approach.

Justin flew to Manchester to meet with the Jodrell Bank observatory in charge. It is one of the finest observatories in the world, especially for tracking meteors and asteroids. People have full trust in what they report.

It was agreed to issue a bulletin confirming the approaching asteroid, also that it would be caught by the gravitational pull of Jupiter like the Shoemaker comet some year ago and no danger to Earth. Newspapers flashed the happy tidings. The world breathed a sigh of relief. But not so for the EW5 team.

"At least people can enjoy the days left, sadly it will be a sudden death sentence, rather than suffer for years waiting for the inevitable." Justin addressed his colleagues.

Discretely Justin visited major observatories worldwide and explained the accuracy of the Jodrell Bank meritorious observation. It was accepted though with some doubt.

Another two months had passed, life on Twin Peak Island continued as usual, except for the four senior astronomers who were counting the days left for the extinction of all life. It was nearly mid night when Dr. Walker decided to step out for a refreshing walk before retiring for the night.

"I will join you, I need it too." Dr. Maki followed him. They strolled in silence, enjoyed the crisp cool air. Dr. Walker murmured almost to himself, "I wonder what Earth would look like after the holocaust, perhaps it will ignite like a fire ball."

"Stop reminding me of the worst things to come, talk something pleasant," Dr. Maki was not in the mood to talk about the inevitable.

They again continued in silence, each lost in thoughts. Decided to sit on a bench, stretched full with their head thrown back staring at the canopy of countless stars, "What a beautiful sight, but up there, there are more infernos that are creating upheavals every second, shaping the scenario that we are witnessing right now which appears peaceful and serene. Earth has survived for four and half billion years, with a few serious misses and strikes, I call it luck and thanks to the giant planets that had swallowed most of the other possible treats. Perhaps the time has come for us to taste the unavoidable.

"What a waste of life, to be extinguished in a jiffy, like someone striking a match in the dark and is snuffed out. We live in a unique world, perhaps nothing like it in our galaxy. We did have near to extinction a few times, but life survived. Not this time." He paused, then added. "Once it is wiped out, it will be millions if not billions of years to start all over again. I wonder if future humans will look like us. What kind of DNA will emerge?"

Dr. Maki stood up, "What morbid thoughts, I have come out to refresh myself not to listen to a doom day lecture. It is obvious what you are saying, why talk about it?"

"Because as scientists we must keep on digging, we may not come out with an answer, but at least we have tried. Someone in the future may pursue it further and come out with some results."

"What are you taking about, what future? In couple of years there will be no one." Dr. Maki put in bluntly.

"Come to think of it, optimistically speaking, *it is* possible for a few or at least one man and one woman to survive somewhere, being at the right place at the right time. Perhaps in a cave or an area least effected by the holocaust. In a few hundred years, population would begin to sprout. The cycle of life would start all over again." Dr. Walker speculated."

"What you are saying makes sense. The possibility of a pair or a few might survive, and that most certainly bring back the human race, all would not lost. We don't have to wait for millions of years, life will spring back in a short time.

"That is how the ball bounces my friend, and we can do nothing about it. Not even with all our technologies combined or the

17

high and mighty who keep flouting their muscles can deviate the oncoming threat an iota of a millimeter. Trillion of dollars are spent on how we can bully our fellow beings, instead, had we spent it wisely on research and technology, we may have had the means to protect our world." Dr. Maki contributed sullenly.

"Dr. Maki, we scientists live in a world of our own, and we are an insignificant minority. We are caught in a domain where logical reasoning does not apply. Let us leave it at that. Right now, not even a miracle can save us, only in fairy tales you have a happy ending."

Dr. Maki got up from the bench, "I think I had enough for one day."

They walked back to the observatory to find Dr. Frank busy at his desk.

"You better wind up, there is always a tomorrow, at least for a couple of more years." Dr. Walker said to Dr. Frank.

A month later, the asteroid was getting near the vicinity of Pluto. The four astronomers worked diligently on its approach. They were in a position to chalk out its trajectory. The result was most alarming.

The four sat in front of a large screen with drawings and sketches spread across in front of them. On the screen was Justin and his EW5 colleagues in London.

Dr. Frank began to explain. "We have now chalked out the exact path of the asteroid. Sadly it will bypass comfortably all the giant planets, but not quite so with Jupiter, close to it but not close enough to be attracted by it. Its trajectory to rendezvous with Earth is roughly somewhere in the Sahara desert. Its impact would be like millions of hydrogen bombs and will turn this beautiful world into a ball of fire, far worse than the one of sixty five millions years ago that killed the dinosaurs and nearly all life." Dr. Frank rested his head in his palms and looked down.

"It looks like our fate is sealed, nothing can be done. Let us live the days that we are left with." Justin consoled.

"I dread the day when we all will be barbequed; what a horrible way to go. I would prefer to take a pill before it happens and avoid that torture." Dr. Maki said softly and sipped his coffee.

"That is a defeatist thought. Live to the very last moment you can breathe. What if there is miracle and the damned thing passes by without touching us or who knows, a knight in a shining armour may step in and save the day." Dr. Rochelle said optimistically.

"Hope you are right Rochelle. Though miracles in this day and age are just a fantasy. Frank, would you please keep me informed if there is a new development, and thank you for the update. Bye for now."

The screen went blank.

Dr. Frank looked at Rochelle, "I liked your optimism, sometimes women say things without realising its implications, for good or bad. Let us hope it is for the good of mankind."

"Very encouraging to think that way Frank, in the old days not long ago we were branded as witches, and our abilities of foresight were misunderstood." She added with a wink.

"Go and enjoy the rest of the day," Dr. Frank said.

Weeks continued to roll by and they kept a strict vigilance.

Late one night Dr. Maki was pinned to the telescope, when he suddenly let out a loud cry that echoed throughout the dome, a burst in Japanese, almost hysterical, he grabbed the telescope with both arms hugged and kissed the eye piece.

The other two colleagues in the room stood motionless and stared at the antics he was performing.

"What's wrong with you, have you gone mad?"

"Better than that, I can't believe what I have seen, come have a look both of you."

Dr. Frank for several long moments pinned his eye to the telescope. Murmured to himself, "Can't see anything extraordinary." There was a pause, "Hold on, I can't see our infamous asteroid."

"You can't because it is no longer there. Something hit it and shattered it to pieces" Dr. Maki proudly shouted back.

Dr. Walker walked up to him and said softly, "Collect yourself and tell us what you have seen?"

"There was that light, like a strong beam hitting the asteroid and minutes later it just shattered. I have recorded the event. You can see it."

On a large screen, the recording was displayed. They saw it over and over again. They went back to the telescope and searched the area where the Inferno asteroid was displaying its might. After two hours they confirmed its explosive demise.

Back in their conference room they waited for Dr. Rochelle to join them. They sipped coffee as they waited.

Dr. Rochelle's entrance was dramatic, with full force she opened the door almost yelling. "It is better be good to ask me to come at this unearthly hour. It is almost three thirty in the morning."

"Cool down, pour yourself some coffee and sit down."

She looked at Dr. Frank quizzically and followed his instructions.

For a few moments he stared at her. Then he just said coolly, "A knight in a shining armour has sent your inferno to hell."

Dr. Rochelle had coined the phrase for the asteroid. She stared at the three and wanted more explanation.

"Yes Mam, the asteroid is no longer with us, somehow it just exploded. You look at the tape and give us your opinion.

She replayed it several times, especially the part of the beam of light hitting it and came out with an amazing analysis.

"To me that beam of light is not light as we know it, more so like a laser blast, some kind of weapon with a mighty power that has shattered it into oblivion."

"Yes, it must be powerful enough to do such a damage. But by whom? We on Earth don't possess such a weapon. It must be by some well-wishers," Dr. Frank said calmly.

"Well-wishers out there near Pluto, let's not talk science fiction stuff, be realistic," Dr. Maki cut in.

Dr. Rochelle was in deep thought, half listening to the speculations the other three were debating on. Then with a loud thump of her fist she startled them.

"Gentlemen, that zap from God knows who, must be by some intelligent beings in our neighbourhood we know nothing about. Let us keep an open mind, we are scientists, there are several moons around Jupiter and Saturn or an unknown planet that has life far more advanced in technology than ourselves. That beam could not have come from nowhere.

"Now may I leave and finish my sleep, meanwhile, do your homework and find our well-wisher." With those words she left leaving the three pinned to their seats thinking about what she had said.

Dr. Maki broke the silence, "What a woman, we never thought of that possibility."

"You are as nutty as she is," Dr. Walker remarked and added, "Intelligent life as we know it, is impossible out there, and cannot exist. Perhaps microbes or bacteria at the outmost."

Dr. Frank, playing with a pencil on the table, commented softly in a low voice. "I tend not to disagree with Dr. Rochelle. Remember Planet X which we have been looking for or some other planet that may exist and know nothing about." He stopped and let his thoughts run freely. Then with a sudden jolt he exclaimed, "I think I got it, the answer is right in front of us. You all remember the aliens who lived on Earth for many years and left suddenly before the Middle East war not many years ago to some planet they called Urna. [i]

"I am now positive they were the ones who gave us another chance. A positive speculation but I will go into that later, now to report to Justin."

Early the next day Dr. Frank called Rochelle, in a sleepy voice she answered, he just said, "Thank you Rochelle, you may have hit the nail on the head." He put the receiver down and on the other end she just shook her head and went back to sleep.

Then he picked the phone and dialed Justin's number.

"Not you again, what is it this time. Have you found another asteroid?"

"Good news this time Justin, the Inferno asteroid has been eliminated."

"What, by whom," Justin exclaimed. "My sleep has gone, might as well tell me more."

Dr. Frank explained the whole story and went on to say, "My guess is that the aliens who left us a few years ago must have done the good deed."

"Do they have such weaponry to destroy such a large object?" Justin asked.

---

[i] The Medallion, a novel by the same author

"If you remember, they are an older civilization, the way they came to Earth after their planet went astray thousands of years ago, and the way they handled the virus crises here using their spaceships.

"I suggest we find the department or the person who dealt with them and try to find a way to communicate with them."

"That is a tall order, but I will do my best." Justin put the telephone receiver down and held to it lost in thought.

Dr. Maki sipped his coffee, thinking. Placing his cup down, looked at his colleagues and suggested, "I think we should be able to find a way to communicate with those aliens, but do we know where they are. Their planet does not appear anywhere, how can we communicate with something which is not there. I am sure London can help.

The next day business as usual, nothing exciting. Both observatories scanned deep space, kept a watchful eye.

Dr. Frank called Justin. "I am doing my best, we have nothing on that planet, give me some time, and I will get back shortly." Was his brief reply and hung up. Justin spent an hour trying to find the special department that handled the aliens when they were on Earth, but to no avail. He decided to call the Prime Minister who might have the where about of that department.

Hours later the Prime Minister called back and told Justin that the department still exists with some skeleton staff and no one is in charge. It is practically non-functional but was told that the last person in charge retired five years ago and his name was Steven Windsor. "But why the sudden interest, is there something you are not telling me?"

Justin had to think of a quick answer, "Can't tell you on the phone, and after you find his where about, let's meet."

Without wasting any time the search for Steven Windsor was on. Minutes later the Prime Minister was told he was on holiday with his family in the Bahamas. He has been just a week into his vacation and was requested to return to London for a few days.

Steven's wife was most unhappy, "Steve, you are a retired man and they have no right to order you around."

"It must be urgent that the Prime Minister himself made the request, I promise to return within the week meanwhile, you have our friend here with you and enjoy the sunshine."

CHAPTER 4

In London Steven Windsor or Steve as called by all, was told about the inferno asteroid and the way it was destroyed. "It must be our friends on Urna that came to our rescue." Was his immediate reaction. "Must thank them for what they have done. Their capabilities are enormous. You mentioned that the EW5 have not been able to locate their planet. How can that be with all the equipment you have down there? We have probes around Mars, how about programing one to scan between Jupiter and Saturn. I do remember, they had mentioned the location of their planet to be somewhere there."

The Prime Minister suggested to Steve to speak to Twin Peak Island, "You can use my office to make that call, we don't want it to get around and strict secrecy must be observed."

Steve got up and said, "Sir, with you permission, I will have to go to my former office and get the coordinates and telephone number they had given me when they left ten years ago. Why don't you and Justin join me, it will be most helpful."

Soon they were at Steve's former office. He knew exactly where to look, in a safe which was not opened since his retirement, lay a file marked in red "Top Secret, for the eyes of the coordinator only."

The Prime Minister and Justin sat patiently as Steve shuffled through the file. "I have found the number but doubtful if it is still functional. They were on their space ship, spoke to them three or four times, the last time was just before reaching their planet, and had trouble with the reception."

Steve looked at Justin, "I understand that you have a state of the art facilities available to you on that island, Let me speak to the man in charge. We can use my phone, our number is not listed and safe to use."

Justin called Dr. Frank, "You remember the planet Urna where our alien friends went just before the war, not long ago, Mr. Steven Windsor who was in charge at the time, is here with me and he was the last person to talk to them when they were about to reach their planet, communication was bad, perhaps you are better equipped. You speak to Steven, he will give you some instructions."

Steven introduced himself briefly and explained Urna's unique position, being shielded by Jupiter, "Its orbit is such that it is difficult to see it from Earth. It is in between Jupiter and Saturn. It is always in opposition with Earth. One of your Martian probes can be programed and sent to that vicinity."

Dr. Frank had a better suggestion, "We have a probe, Charon is just about to reach Jupiter's vicinity, on its way to Pluto, may be a better idea to change its course to orbit Jupiter, it would then be easy and quicker to spot Urna. Once we find it will call you."

Charon spotted the elusive planet. Steve and Justin flew to the island. On the flight Justin studied some of the files. "Who is this Ayond, was he in charge?"

"Ayond is a she and a very pleasant lady. She looks very human, in fact all the aliens on that planet are like us. You must complete reading the files. I just hope she is still there. There is also a separate file on the Earth people who had left with her."

They were received at Twin Peaks Island by Dr. Frank and his colleagues and were taken on a tour of the two observatories. They were briefed on the up to date most highly sophisticated radio telescopes and computerized systems, "You have all this on this island and nothing can escape you. That is how you spotted the asteroid," Steven commented.

"Yes Mr. Steven, except for your friends on Urna who are tucked away between Jupiter and Saturn that is why it escaped from our view." Dr. Maki said.

"You are right, but now with Charon you have spotted it. From what I understand that you have already made a full study of the planet. Love to have a look."

"Yes of course Mr. Steven." Dr. Maki replied.

"I have a request to make, let us do away with formalities, please call me Steve as all my friends do, and I shall address you by your first names, if it is okay with you all."

Steve narrated his association with the aliens when they were on Earth, he mentioned Ayond as the person he dealt with, and explained the function of their highly sophisticated computer they call the Supreme High and how they came about to possessing it. Found it on a remote uninhabited world where life became extinct due to some natural catastrophe. He ended by telling them how they survived their ordeal when their planet broke away from its binary system and drifted freely as a rouge planet in space and how the Supreme High guided and controlled it. They found Earth by accident and settled there and made it their home. That was about fifteen thousand years ago. They left us recently about ten years ago.

"Should we meet them again, I will bring them to your facility, they will be happy to meet you all. And," he paused for a moment, "You can tell your story how you spotted the asteroid and how you saw its demise."

The next few days they laboured with all possible means to communicate, but only got static signals. Urna was orbiting Jupiter as one of its other moons, and Charon was as its satellite.

"I just hope that the communication contact used ten years ago is still functional. I spoke to them while they were on their space ship on their way to Urna. I hope the number has not changed, but we will keep trying."

While they waited Charon displayed Urna's surface, saw water canals, some structures and several satellites rotating around it.

"With those satellites they should be able to receive us, just hope the telephone number still works." Justen remarked.

Steve sat in front of a large screen showing Urna in full view, behind him Frank and his colleagues stood motionless, while he repeatedly continued to call.

No response.

"Hello Urna, come in, this is Steve from Earth." He kept repeating and waited for the hours to pass for his signal to reach and should there be response, more time in receiving it. He called again and again.

"It is going to be a long wait, can someone please get me a strong cup of coffee," Steve requested with his eyes pinned to the screen.

Rochelle dashed to the coffee pot at the far end of the room. "One cup coming up, anyone else?" She asked, no one responded. They were tense or did not hear her.

Pin drop silence filled the room as all remained pinned to the ground, the only sound was Steve's coffee cup hitting the saucer. Many hours passed when suddenly a faint crackling noise came through a speaker. The static and crackling noise continued to fill the room, then there was a coughing sound. They all exchanged glances and waited. Minutes passed and the silence was frustrating.

"Hallo Steve, good to hear from you, we were just thinking of you, I have some good news," The message stopped but Steve immediately answered, "Is that you Ayond, what news of our friends, Sam and the team?"

Hours later, "Ayond here, Sam and his friends are well and are with me right now, we have a surprise for you Steve, we are all coming to Earth soon, to be exact in less than three months. The Supreme High, if you remember him has ordered us to make the visit. In fact we are on a space ship heading your way, left Urna days ago, that's why you managed to get the connection. Keep the kettle boiling, dying for an Earth cup of tea."

Steve adjusted himself to the chair and leaned closer to the microphone, "Tell me Ayond, the asteroid that was heading to

Earth, did you have anything to do with its destruction, if so, we are indebted to the people of Urna."

They waited impatiently for the hours to pass, "I'll tell you all about it when we meet. It is difficult to talk right now, be patient and by the way about our Facility, I hope it still exists. You have the keys, can you please check it out and do the needful. I will talk to you again when we are in the vicinity. Give me you contact numbers in London."

Steve did so and also that of the Twin Island's. He wished her a safe trip.

They all clapped and Frank put in, "Very impressive Steve, she still remembers you and what facility was she talking about."

"That is their residential Facility somewhere outside London, they had it for thousands of years, all underground. You have to see it to believe what it looks like.

Steve explained and added, "Justin, you must invite her here to meet your astronomers."

"Will certainly do." He replied.

The next day Steve and Justin left the Island

CHAPTER 5

In London the EW5 met with the Prime Minister and Steve. They were impressed with Steve handling the situation. "You seemed to know them well," The Prime Minister said appreciably.

"Very well, you all must have read my reports to the then Prime Minister about my association with them and the fiasco at the United Nations which led them to leave Earth permanently."

"Yes, I did and passed them on to the EW5." The Prime Minister said and added, "Well done Steve, I think you better join the service again, the country needs you."

"Yes sir, but before that, can I finish my holiday in the Bahamas, my wife is waiting for me. I will be back in London in a month's time, we have plenty of time before they arrive."

"Just one more question, why do you think she is coming back, especially after the unruly treatment she got at the United Nations?"

Steve shuffled in his chair and looked directly at the Prime Minister, "Perhaps to tell us about the asteroid. She and her alien entourage were most friendly and wanted the best for us, despite the reception she got at the United Nations, the aliens eradicated the virus which took almost three billion lives. They were more concerned, they just love us, after all Earth was their home too for many years, and those people from here that accompanied her would be glad to come back."

"And perhaps ask something in return?" The Prime Minister said casually.

"They are givers not takers, they want the best for us and want to see us happy." Steve said.

"On the contrary, they will be shocked to see a different world full of sickness, disease and poverty. The non-vibrant life that we have become for some reason, cities lay in ruins and our economic and industrial deterioration." Justin remarked and added, "Tell us briefly why you think they love our world when they have their own?"

"It is all in the reports, no harm in briefing you to get more familiar with their background. They came here fifteen thousand year ago not by choice, their rouge planet happened to enter our solar system when humans were in their early stage of development, they assisted discretely in many ways. You might say they formed a bond and felt they had a right of abode. On top of their hierarchy is the Supreme High whom they hold in utmost veneration, although it is a highly sophisticated computer, they refer to it as a *him*. He is the final word. Anyway, they just love this world for its beauty and complex life forms and still consider it as their home, after all many generation of aliens were born here." Steve concluded.

"Very interesting, in fact they do have an equal right to be here as we do, we must plan a befitting reception. I hope they can help us to get out of the chaos we are in and back to order. If I may, can you spend some more time for the benefit of the five members of the EW5 and perhaps Justin would enjoy it too. Why did they leave their planet in the first place?" The Prime Minister requested.

"Glad to sir, they did not leave their planet at will, they were forced to. As I said, their planet Urna drifted freely in space because of some astronomical anomaly that shunted it out of its binary system. It was their Supreme High who guided the ill-fated planet, somehow he guided its stability and sailed it through the emptiness of space. They found Earth by chance, decided to ferry as many as possible, the rest were left behind. They fist landed on the plains between the five rivers that is known today as the Indus Valley, in what is now Pakistan. Unknown to them, Urna miraculously was caught by the sun and place it into orbit in our solar system. It was much later they got to know that their planet was safe and sound between Jupiter and Saturn, but preferred to stay on Earth. That all started some fifteen thousand years ago.

"As far as the Earth men are concerned, they had an artefact or a medallion which the aliens had misplaced, with that, to activate a device which the aliens had hidden in a pyramid, with a message to mankind to tell them of their stay on Earth, should they not be there when discovered. The humans assisted them to retrieve that device which was found some years before by the Egyptian authorities and remained safe in a museum. To cut the story short, when it was retrieved and the message therein was read to the world at the United Nations; hoping that the humans would appreciate the contributions made by the aliens, instead she was scoffed and jeered, and her presentation was labelled as a hoax.

They felt offended and decided to leave as it was not worthy to stay, and let the human race face what was coming to them, for the better or worse. It was then the Earth people who assisted in retrieving the device were offered to join them to go to their world, which they had accepted.

"One more interesting part to add. With the aliens there is a woman, she is from Earth but not human, belongs to a different species, called Jinn. I leave you to ponder over it. When you meet her she will introduce herself more appropriately. In a nut shell this is what I have to say for the time being. Please read all the files and get the full picture."

Justin and the other listeners and were dazed.

"It is an unbelievable storey, imagine aliens living under our roof and we had no clue of their presence. Anyhow, let's get back into the present." The Prime Minister said, "We are today in a world gone crazy, people are not behaving rationally, law and order has gone topsy-turvy as if something in the air that makes them act chaotic and unruly. We just don't know what is causing it. And, to top it all the freak dehumanized terrorists, how did they suddenly materialise? I wonder if your alien friends can shed some light on all this."

Steve's thoughts drifted away, his mind was elsewhere. "I hope they agree to help us, they can do a lot to put things in order. Their policy is not to interfere with Earth problems, but seeing the state of affair they might condescend to do the needful after getting clearance from …. " He was interrupted by Justin. "Are you with us Steve, you seem to be lost in thoughts, how about asking your friend to address the United Nations ….."

Before he could finish, Steve raised a hand, "Sorry Justin, it was tried before, she will not do it, after the insults she had received ten years ago. I have to tackle the issue in a different way. Let's wait and see her mood. Perhaps she would come out with a solution.

"In a few days they would be close and communication would be better. I will prepare the grounds for her sympathetic response. Meanwhile, I will inspect their Facility and make it habitable once again, and of course the hanger, to accommodate their ship."

CHAPTER 6

The EW5 Head Quarters was on a full alert, any incoming messages were to be communicated to Steve and Justin, night or day.

Ayond's space ship was about half a million miles from the moon, chatting with her Earth colleagues, when she was interrupted and alerted by a communication's officer. He spotted a space ship coming towards them, and had the markings of Xanthum, an old adversary, a reptilian race going back to the time they had first landed on Earth fifteen thousand years ago, who used humans as labour to mine gold and salt.

"What are they doing here, I thought we made it clear to them long ago that they keep out of Earth," she exclaimed, and promptly ordered her ship's captain to intercept.

Soon they were at close range, a warning was communicated to stop, to be boarded and inspected. The Xanthumian ship ignored, and tried to maneuver an escape. Ayond's ship responded with a blinding ray of light that surrounded the vessel, causing it to neutralise its movements and it came to a halt.

Ayond stared at the screen, and asked the Xanthumian captain as to what they were doing in this sector of space, and reminded him of the ban imposed on them long time ago. Then asked him if they were coming from Earth and what cargo they were carrying.

No response, "I know you can see and hear me, your silence mean nothing to me, I can blow your ship into pieces, but I will spare you to take back a message to your commander Xanthum; tell him, only recently we knew his location in the solar system, but we ignored him, but when it comes to visiting Earth, we have to act. And, also remind him, if he is not aware, that his ancestors were prohibited to fly beyond Jupiter." She communicated in a foreign language.

On the screen her colleagues watched what was happening.

The Xanthumian captain came on to the screen and condescendingly said, "You may send your inspectors, but our commander would be most angry by your action."

A shuttle took five of inspectors and they boarded the Xanthumian vessel.

The moment they were in, Ayond send a blast of gelatine like substance that enveloped the adversary's ship in a bubble.

Ayond informed the captain that his ship was completely paralyzed, any attempt to fire on her ship, would cause it to disintegrate.

The Earth companions stood amazed and watched. They could not understand the dialogue that transpired, as it was in a language foreign to them.

The inspectors came on the screen, "We have found gold, tons of it." While they were in communication with Ayond, and the other four inspectors had their weapons aimed at the crew, one of the

Xanthumian's rushed to a panel to fire at Ayond's vessel, as he did, the entire vessel exploded and its fragments remained suspended within the bubble.

"I had warned them, that is what you get when trying to get smart. I am sorry for the loss of our men."

At that moment she was alerted by the approach of another Xanthumian ship. All had witnessed the scene of minutes before, and the pile of junk within the bubble that lay hopelessly suspended in the void.

Without waring the adversary let loose a barrage of bolts of lightning strikes. Ayond's ship had its shield up, and were deflected away harmlessly. In return, she just pressed a button, struck the antagonist with a thin beam of light and melted it down in an instant.

Ayond left the controls and went back to join her Earth friend who witnessed the entire show on a screen.

"That was that," she said and sat down. "I suspect that they had returned to Earth no sooner after we left ten years ago. Now they got what they deserve. I have to clean up their operation down there, before we meet our friends," Ayond said, then added, "Why the grim faces, you all seem distressed at what has happened here."

Sam just shook his head and replied softly, "In a way yes, loss of life on the second ship, it was inhumane."

"I am sorry you looked at it that way, in your world I thought the act of force and violence is the order of the day. What I have done goes back many years ago when we discovered an alien race infamous in your solar system who plundered and enslaved your people to mine gold and take it away to their world. They were there before us, settled on one of Jupiter's moons which has conditions same as their world.

"Their home planet is somewhere in the Cygnet constellation, their planet was dying and most of them were sent out in search of a new home, some found your solar system and chose one of Jupiter's moon Io, an ideal location and at the same time surveyed other planets, found Earth, rich in gold, a mineral they use for the manufacture energy. But with our arrival, we had to ban them from visiting this planet and avoid flying beyond Jupiter. When we left ten years ago, they took the opportunity to come back. We just hope they have not done any serious damage and enslaved people.

"You will witness our wrath when we will annihilate them once and for all. We love your planet as we do ours. Not forgetting your contribution to our world, and the introduction of the English language and some of the good cultures."

David came in quietly and stood beside them. "Just chatting with Sam, my old and trusted friend," Ayond said to David, "I owe it to him for introducing us, and remember our first meeting at the coffee shop when he had the medallion. I also remember my first meeting with Sam when he walked into our shop to buy an old folding camera. It was then I saw in him a potential, or better still a person who would someday be useful to us.

"Furthermore, I am also grateful to him for introducing you, Jim and Daniel and made us into a team," Ayond looked around, "Sam where is your wife Aishtra?"

Soon they were all together and began to talk of the days when they were on Earth, "I wonder what the situation is right now, after their wars. The whole place must be in a mess. And not forgetting the possibility of the Xanthumian occupation and what harm they may have done to enslave some of the countries," Ayond added sadly.

"Excuse me Ayond, who exactly are the Xanthumians and where do they come from?" David asked.

"That is a long story David, I was just talking about them to Sam, in a nut shell they are an evil race of reptilians, sub human evolved from reptilian ancestor, imagine a life form developed over millions of years from a dinosaur-like ancestry, like you might say humans developed from chimpanzees. They are aggressive by nature, selfish and have no respect for any other forms of life.

"As I have mentioned earlier, they come from an obscure planet in the Cygnet Constellation, their sun was dying and they decided to leave in search of a new home. One of the ships with their leader landed on Io, one of the moons of Jupitar and from there they surveyed all the planets in the solar system. Earth was chosen as it had people and is rich in minerals.

"When we came to Earth our first job was to remove them and put a ban on their travelling beyond Jupiter, they tried to return, our answer was a lesson they would not forget, destroyed most of their ships, only some got away. For all the years we stayed on Earth, they never dared to come back, but must have discretely kept a watch and when we left, ten years ago, they grabbed the opportunity and returned. Just hope they have not done much harm," Ayond concluded.

"That is quite a story, imagine we have been visited by aliens going back thousands of years, perhaps there were others who visited us. Our ancestors created some of our legends about monsters and demons from tell-tale narratives perhaps based on ET visitations," Jim quietly murmured.

"You may be right Jim, and probably some religions associated those stories with gods, devils and a place called hell," Daniel added and continued, "Since my association with you all especially Ayond and Aishtra, I have removed the curtain off my eyes which blinded me to see reason and face the truth. I, as most of my fellow men and women have literary lived in false beliefs, based on the sayings of uninformed scholars based on hearsays and legendary folklore."

"Well said Daniel, you were a man of God and ran a church, to hear you say this, it bewilders me," Sam said, then continued, "But what you have done on Urna bewilders me more. Though you have no church or Gospel to preach, yet you have become very popular with the masses who came to hear your wisdom on how beautiful life is and the splendor of knowledge, a gift that can come only from the environment we are blessed with."

"You have put it philosophically, what Daniel has achieved goes beyond a preacher." Jim complimented.

"Enough of that, how about you Aishtra, are happy to return to Earth. After all it is your home too," Ayond changed the subject.

Aishtra moved close to Sam, and put her hand on his head, "My home is with Sam now, as far as my ancestral home with my fellow beings, I have forgotten it. As a child the only home I had is with Ayond as a mother who brought me up when I survived the crash and lost my parents, in due course I became a new person and now living on Urna and married to a human."

"Yes but you are a still a Jinn as they call your race on Earth," Jim said.

She thought for some moments and added, "True I was born a Jinn and still have all the capabilities of a Jinn, our children will perhaps have some of those traits, and future generation might turn into some new form of entity. For now, I and all of us here are from a place called Urna. Visitors to Earth, a place once we called home."

"Well said Aishtra," David said.

They were interrupted by the communication officer, "Soon we will be approaching Earth's moon. We are going to slow down to low speed, what are your orders?"

"Just stay on the far side of the moon, we don't want Earth to see us as yet. Wait for further instructions," Ayond said and followed him to the bridge.

CHAPTER 7

Ayond returned shortly with a wide smile, "Have a look at Earth before we dock on the far side, it looks lovely. So innocent and majestic, can you imagine that little rock is teaming with life, from the lowest form to intelligent beings. That little speck is in infinite space, should it suddenly ignite, there will be a flash, breaking it into fragments, leaving a void of darkness, and a passing space ship may not know that once a beautiful world existed in that emptiness between the two planets, Mars and Venus."

"Well put Ayond, it is a pity such a unique world is in an array of dead planets of a solar system, located in the boon-docks of the Galaxy, and should meet such a fate. How I wish the people on Earth can witness this scene, it will surely change their views on how to respect that Rock, we call home," David remarked.

Jim shook his head, "Nothing can change them, once they get back, their attitude of the powerful and mighty will rule again. What the people need is someone with a stick which is the only way peace can be cultivated into that scheme of things."

Daniel stood alone beside a window. "How beautiful, how beautiful," he kept repeating. He thought of God, "He must be watching it too, and He must be knowing what goes on there. Though the *good people* he sent did some good, but still not as much good as He wanted it to be. Why does He not visit this beautiful gem we call Earth? May be he knows that nothing will change. It is perhaps a lost cause."

Sam came up behind him, "I can guess what you are thinking, that rock you are looking at is no more your concern. What you are doing on Urna is the true nature of enlightenment. Come and join us we are having a drink.

They spent hours chatting and enjoyed the company of some female personnel working on the ship. Ayond was gone for some time. She and some senior officers were sitting in a closed room planning their entry to Earth, and the steps to be taken in case of any military confrontation with the Xanthumains.

It was the next day that Ayond met the group and made a surprise announcement. Without hesitation they all answered with one voice.

"Yes we love to."

"As you have no training to walk on the moon, you will have to use a rope hooked to each one of you, and walk in single file until you return to the premises. The gravity inside the base is Earth like, but outside is only one sixth."

One of the small ships brought them into a crater. They felt a slight vibration as the ship descended gently into a dark pit. At the bottom they disembarked and were taken on a tour of the facility. Showed them rooms where the residents worked and lived. Then were taken to a greenhouse like set up filled with vegetation, fruits and vegetables. Small androids busied watering plants, some were digging and testing the soil, a few walked about as if surveying the work done. The androids ignored the tourist like onlookers and went about their work. Lights flooded the entire garden as if it was sunshine in a tropical place.

In a room filled with equipment and screens, "From here we monitor Earth and relay it to our headquarters on Urna." Someone explained.

They walked back near to the entrance gate, and were dressed in space suits, "Now do not forget not to leave the rope under any circumstances, just follow the instructions of your guide, and enjoy the tour." The person in charge of the base advised.

They stepped into an elevator that took them to the surface. They were hooked to a cable and in a single file they cautiously threaded on the lunar surface. At the creator's edge they walked up on what looked like a paved gradient. Their guide's watchful eyes were fixed on them, and assisted some to keep their balances. After almost an hour of regimented excursion, Sam discretely unbuckled his umbilical cord and went about freely kicking up dust and jumping around. He darted upwards a few feet and fell back, and repeated his antics several times. While the guide approached to buckle him with the others, Jim and Daniel freed themselves and joined Sam.

The teenage spirit rose high within them, kicked dust, hopped up and down, scooped up sand and threw it up high. David watched and shouted encouraging words to do better. The guide was not amused, and with an authoritative voice and hand threating gestures brought them to order. With his voice still ringing in their helmets, they humbly condescended and followed him back to the creator. They solemnly descended through the pit and on to their vehicle to take them back to the mother ship.

After the team got cleaned up, they met with Ayond. "I understand your young strokes of fun got the better of some of you, good to have fun sometimes, it brings the youthful spirit in you, though it was a risk you should not have taken.

"Now I am going to tell you that we will not communicate with Earth until we find out what is happening down there, I am sending a team to check if any Xanthumains are still present. Three of our smaller war ships will survey the situation and take any action necessary. There will be no marking on our ships, they will do their job and slip out."

CHAPTER 8

Early dawn, three small saucers shaped crafts headed towards Earth, to start their operation from Africa. Detection beams would expose any alien activity. The metal of their ships and their facilities would easily detect their presence.

Near about South Africa two Xanthumains ships just began to ascend when they spotted the three saucer shaped crafts, without warning opened fire. Their detection system maneuvered the assault and flew back acrobatically over the large transport vessels, and reciprocated with a shower of deadly fire, sent both plummeting out of control and explode.

The Xanthumains base was in full alert and before their ships and men could assemble, hell fire broke loose, reduced them to ashes. Similar facilities were detected in neighbouring Namibia and Angola. A fierce battle raged for some time to the success of Ayond's war machines. Luckily all the Xanthumian bases were in the desert and sparsely populated.

The three ships combed the entire continent and found no enemy presence. Scrambled to different parts of the world, over North and South America, Asia and Australia, all was clear.

Next was to study the general conditions of life and social status on the planet. Their findings was not encouraging. Pathetic scenes from war torn countries lay in ruins where the inhabitants lived in makeshift tents or within broken down buildings, all in the Middle East, North Africa and some parts of Asia. By night, fires over the Persian Gulf gave a sad story, the oil rich wells were ablaze, and dark clouds of smoke covered the entire area and further east into Afghanistan and beyond.

Europe, Russia and the Americas were not as vibrant as should be, and the general look gave a picture of a stagnant social order. The human race looked as if they were mesmerized, people go about their business with solemn faces.

"I can't make head or tail of their reports." Ayond's worried expression showed on her face, "It is perhaps that the Xanthumains had put a spell on places they want to control. That is an old form of governess, used in some worlds, we call it collective hypnoses using your terminology. They may have put a satellite to that effect that causes lassitude. We'll get rid of it. I am sure those creatures will return some day, but before that, get rid of them once and for all. Completely wipe them out on their home grounds, and you all will witness some real cosmic fireworks. I am sure the Supreme High would approve."

"Speaking of the Supreme High, how can we communicate with him, he is so far from us…" David did not finish his sentence when Ayond interrupted,

"I should have told you before we left, when we built this massive space ship we needed a new form of guiding and communication systems. The Supreme High with the help of the Guardian helped us to build a miniature of himself to enable us to communicate with him. It will be his eyes and ears so to speak to watch over us.

"On this ship we just refer to it as Argos, from the word Argoshtak coined for the enigmatic occasion when for three days Urna is surrounded around its equator with a belt of white misty vapour, changing gradually to several concentric circles, the colours of the rainbow, in the middle of it a large oval buckle-shaped concentration of purplish cloud like formation with flashes of light churning within its parameter.

"Traditionally we believe its presence is a good omen, and on those special three days, once in three of our years we celebrates its affluence and wisdom that it bestows upon us. We don't know how or what causes it. We only know for certain, it brings prosperity everywhere. You have lived on our planet for about ten years, but missed the three occasions this phenomena appeared. We were then out exploring the solar system. But if we are lucky to be back to Urna before the next Argoshtak, you will witness its spectacle.

"Argos, whatever we do, and the ship's behaviour is reported to his boss the Supreme High. Will introduce you to it, after we land."

"How strange you have the name Argos in your world, on Earth there is a city by that name in Greece. It is very ancient and a prosperous city to this day," David put in.

"Tell us about this ship," Sam requested.

Ayond proudly said, "It is perhaps the biggest ship ever built by us. Its shape is a bit odd, more or less like two tubs on each other with some curves here and there to make it pleasant to look at. It is about eleven hundred feet long and two hundred feet wide. It has a maximum speed of 500,000 per hour, we use that speed on inter planetary travel. From the moon to Earth we'll go at much lower speed. Its source of power is too complicated for you to understand, in a nut shell, it is based on light.

"It has one extra feature, we can turn it invisible. It has weaponry your world can't imagine. It can wipe out a city like New York with just one blast. I can go on for hours telling you what this great ship is capable of. Can you guess who designed it?"

They shook their heads.

"Our Supreme High and the Guardian, both are great engineers and architects too. As we are talking the Supreme High is listening to our conversation. Nothing can be hidden from him. If he wishes, this ship can be blown to pieces. There are external sensors which also communicate to him all what is going on the outside.

"Tell us something more about the Guardian, we all had met him briefly on Earth and a few times on Urna, but never got to know him." Jim asked.

"He is as knowledgeable as the Supreme High but to a lesser extent, remember he was made by him. We never questioned his authority, as all his instructions come from his maker. Enough of that, now let's all go up to the bridge and enjoy our departure for our old home."

They were received by the senior members of the crew, who were waiting for Ayond's arrival.

"Be seated," she said as they got up to greet her, and asked her companions to do the same.

"I want to brief you on the situation on Earth," she addressed her crew. "The Xanthumains have been eradicated down there, but their effect of collective hypnosis will take time to wear off after we get rid of the satellite causing it. But that does not concern us at this time. Our friend Steve sounded normal when I spoke to him.

"For the first few days, we will study the up to date position on Earth and consult Argos for what action to take. This time I am sorry to say, Earth people will have to listen to us, even if by force. It will not be like the old days when we left them alone. You all have studied our files of how we lived on Earth for thousands of years and the indirect help we gave in farming, some scientific knowledge, music, arts and many other fields. Some of you have joined our fleet recently and are not familiar with life down there, your senior colleagues can help you.

"It is a beautiful world, but some of the people down there can't appreciate that splendour, they are busy in creating divisions and chaos, and settle their differences by acts of war. All for political and financial ends. Many were roped in innocently or with hidden agendas, resulting in chaos infecting the rest like a plaque.

"Now prepare for departure, we should land in the United Kingdom around noon. But first let us greet and enjoy the grandeur of that blue world as it comes to view. Drift gently from the far side of the moon and stay put for a while. I have arranged to play a portion of the first movement of Tchaikovsky's violin concerto, a befitting gesture, while we watch it materialise.

They all gathered near windows and looked at the speckled crater surface. The ship began to drift gently, the music began to fill the cabin. Emotions began to overwhelm the onlookers as a blueish ball size world came to full view. They remained pinned, thoughts ran, remembered days gone by when once they cherished the sounds of children playing, the busy streets, the laughter of friends, and the pleasant evenings spent.

"Will it be the same when we touch down?" Sam thought.

Gradually the music faded, but all remained still. Ayond discretely wiped off the tears from her clouded eyes, "I will call Steve to arrange for our landing," she said and walked away.

"Hello Earth, calling Steven," she kept repeating. No response. "Perhaps it is too early in the morning for them. I will try the other number."

A female voice, "I am Rochelle from an observatory, whom am I speaking to?"

Ayond introduced herself.

"I shall alert Steve that you have called, you can call him back in London in about an hour." Rochelle said and gave Justin's office telephone number. After several tries she managed to wake him and conveyed Ayond's message. In turn Steve contacted Justin.

Shortly the two met at the EW5 office and waited for Ayond's call.

Crisp and clear came her voice, "Sorry to drag you out of bed, I am parked near the moon, I thought of getting your permission to fly in."

"What a surprise, of course you are most welcome to come home. In how many days." Ayond interrupted him, "Not days, just hours say about noon. Tell me if it is safe to land near about our old hanger area. We need a large space, our ship is about eleven hundred feet long and two feet wide."

Steve did not answer, he was confused, thought for a moment, "That open area near the hangers is still vacant and under our supervision, yes, your ship should fit in there, I will send people to prepare for your landing." He gave his cell phone number and asked her to call on arrival.

"Good, see you soon. Meet us at the grounds, make sure the grounds are free from onlookers, you know what I mean. Bye for now."

Ayond hung up, but Steve was not at ease. He looked at Justin, "I can't imagine an eleven hundred feet long space ship landing and not attract public attention."

"You may have to get some help from the authorities to have such a large corridor to keep the locals out, you better hurry, make your calls. I will inform the Prime Minister. He might like to join us," Justin said.

Steve made a few phone calls and within an hour security was in place near the hangers where the aliens had housed their ships ten years ago.

"Sooner or later the public will spot it and that will be a big problem to keep them off bound," Steve murmured.

Just before noon the Prime Minister arrived.

"Very good of you to have come," Steve addressed the Prime Minister to which he replied, "I think it is a matter of utmost importance that I receive our guests, they have travelled millions of miles and for me just a few. Steve, as you know them personally, please do the introduction."

They waited inside the old hanger along with some security staff and their vehicles. Time passed and no sign of a spaceship. Then suddenly Steve's phone rang, "Hello, yes it is me Ayond, where are you, we have arrived?

He paused and said loudly, "Where? Where are you, can't see a thing."

Ayond chuckled, then added, "Just come outside."

They walked cautiously and looked in all directions, the place was empty then all of a sudden they saw some human forms materializing in a straight line coming out of nowhere. Steve hurried towards them, he recognise Ayond and her team, Sam, David, Jim, Daniel and Aishtra. Justin and the Prime Minister trailed behind cautiously.

Ayond embraced and shook hands, "Steve, it has been a long time, we landed about half an hour ago, and waited for your arrival."

"Where have you come from, are you real or ghosts, where is your ship?"

"Right here, behind us, you can't see it because it is invisible."

"I'll be damned," Steve exclaimed.

"Aren't you going to introduce us to your friends?" Ayond said extending her hand to the bewildered entourage that stood behind him.

"Forgive me, this is our Prime Minister and Justin the head of our space research."

Ayond then introduced her team. Steve was the last to shake hands with them and added, "Urna did you good, you all don't look a day older than when you left, and by the way, where is Saeed the Egyptian, and Jim's wife, are they not with you?"

"He decided not to come, deeply involved in organizing a new museum that will host all the Earthly artifacts, books, photographs and maps. To familiarize our people with your world as it will be part of our curriculum in schools and colleges, and Jim's wife preferred to stay behind." Ayond explained.

David looked up at the clear sky, stretched both arm high above his head and took a deep breath, "Ahhhh, nice to be on good old Earth."

They walked to the hanger. Ayond said, "Now look outside I will show you our ship. But first put on these glasses.

The Prime Minister had his mouth wide open, "It is massive, as big as an aircraft carrier."

"If you like Your Excellency, you can have a tour of the ship."

"I would love to," he said softly.

"Love to," Justin said and started walking.

They entered the ship through a small door. "In here we have our smaller ships, "So that is what a flying saucer looks like," the Prime Minister murmured to himself. Then added looking at Ayond, "Is it true that these little ships can do what we have been told and as we see them in the movies?"

"Much more Your Excellency, We will arrange a ride for you and your friends someday. Now follow me," Ayond said pointing to an elevator. "We will start with the top floor."

They entered a room lined with what looked like electronic equipment with multi-coloured dials and crystal knobs of different colours and sizes.

"This is the weaponry area, the screens have a 360 degrees visual of the outside, all controlled electronically. You don't see any weapons anywhere, on the outside or inside. When needed, they would discreetly emerge from all directions. This ship has the power to split your moon in two."

They moved to a lower floor, "This what you may call the bridge. The whole ship is controlled from here." There were only instruments and screens. Someone asked, "Don't you have windows to look outside, does it not gets monotonous to look at instruments all the time with no outside view?"

"Yes we have windows, used at times to give us a view of space or survey a landscape," Ayond pressed a button and the entire front and sides of the ship slid open. They could see for miles, farms, buildings and people.

"What a view, I could sit for hours admiring the beauty before me," Justin said as he leaned against a widow.

The next floor, "This is our living area and the floor below is for the staff's. Shortly they descended to the bottom.

Steve put a question to Ayond, "How many floors are there, I forgot to count."

"Seven, you have seen only three, the other lower four levels are living and storage area for a lot of necessities that we require during our long journeys in space. Nothing of your interest. And of course here on the ground floor is where we keep our smaller vehicles which you call flying saucers.

The Prime Minister thanked Ayond and left. Justin accompanied him.

Steve, Ayond, her crew and colleagues drove to their old residential Facility. "It is as good as when you left it, what I suggest is that you all take rest for a couple of days and we meet at Justin's office and show you what we have. Nothing as fancy as your ship, but the best we have." Steve put in politely.

CHAPTER 9

Ayond accompanied by her crew took over the Facility which they had built and occupied during their stay on Earth for many years. During their absence, Steve, before his retirement had arranged a team of security personnel to look after it.

Sam and his colleagues occupied the rooms which they had lived in when they were guests at the start of their association with the aliens. Aishtra, though she was married to Sam had to occupy her official quarters as an officer. Ayond was in full command of the Facility and resided in a room adjacent to the section where the Supreme High was located.

Going around the Facility, she was satisfied with its security and the comfort of her crew. Back in her room, from a small box measuring eighteen by ten inches, she took out Argos, the Supreme High in miniature, carried it and walked up to where the large cube of the Supreme High had rested. On a table she placed it, connected it with a few wires that lay on the ground. Second later she was talking to Argos.

"I can see you Ayond, it is good to feel I am alive again. Soon I will be connected to the Supreme High and communication will be restored as usual." When they finished she picked a golden foil and covered it.

In her room she sat at a desk with a large screen. She busied herself with instruments, "All are working well, time to rest." She said to herself and pressed a button. "Yes Ayond, what can I do for you?" Aishtra replied.

"Can you go and check on David and the rest if they need anything. I will meet you and them tomorrow."

Aishtra was happy to go as she will also meet Sam. She wasted no time, in minutes she was at David's room.

As he opened the door, she was greeted by the whole team who were partying, and some were singing.

"Come in Aishtra, we are celebrating our coming home again, join in," Sam voice rang loudly as he ran up to her. They danced for a while, the others clapped keeping up with the music. It lasted for about an hour. Sam and Aishtra slipped away to the garden while the rest slumbered on the sofas and David's bed.

They were awakened by an attendants who brought in their dinner. They ate in silence and no sooner they had finished they parted to their rooms.

The next day, late afternoon Ayond and Aishtra came to David's room and asked the others to join in.

Ayond started, "It seem like yesterday that we were here, and the Facility is as good as we left it, thanks to Steve. Of course we are missing our Guardian and the Supreme High. But I do have the miniature Supreme High, Argos is already fixed and alive."

"We did not see him getting into the Facility, how and who?" Sam asked

"I carried him in a box, he is so small in size that none of you suspected. Anyhow he is here, and we will need him during our stay."

"You keep addressing Argos as him, why so?" David asked.

"Out of respect, as he represents his master." She replied then added, Sam and Daniel, please contact your cousin Michael, better still, go and meet him. A car will be at your disposal, and if you want to drive, feel free but be back in two days.

"As for you David and Jim decide what you want to do."

David shook his head, "I have no one to meet, and tried to contact my sons after we arrived, and some one answered but had no idea about the previous occupants. I have no way of finding out where have they moved to. It looks that my connection with this worlds ended when I left ten years ago."

Jim opted to go to his house. "I will go to my old house, the chances are my sons may have moved out of France. My wife is on Urna she would have loved to meet them, but I'll do it for her."

"Well then it is settled, see you all in two days," Ayond got up to go and added, "Aishtra can you see to it that they get their transportation and feel free if you want to join them.

Sam looked at David who sat with his head down, "David why don't you come with me and Daniel, it will be an outing and we will have some company."

David agreed and Aishtra decided to join them.

They walked up to a garage and selected cars of their choice. Drove and waited for a panel to slide open, no sooner they emerged to the surface and were on the highway, the cars shot off like bullets.

"Take it easy Sam, we are in no hurry, we have two days," Aishtra said uncomfortably balancing on the back seat with Daniel.

They reached Michael's house. It was dark, no lights on the outside. Sam rang the bell and waited. Minutes later he saw a light come on in a room and he rushed to a window, peeped through and saw a shadowy figure walked clumsily towards the door. They waited, the door opened with a squeak.

"Yes," a feeble voice greeted him.

"Is that you Michael?"

"Yes, what can I do for you?" The man asked in a hardly audible voice.

"It is me, Sam your cousin."

Michael looked at him up and down, "No it can't be, you have not aged a bit, but you had gone to some planet years ago."

Sam opened his arms and were locked in an embrace, "Let's go inside and explain everything to you. I have Daniel and David with me, do you remember them, and Aishtra my wife."

Soon they were seated and Aishtra was the first to speak. "We met briefly once but that was long ago when Sam invited us to your house. You were young and strong, you have aged and why are you living alone?

"It is a long story, but before that let's have some refreshments. Sam can you do the honours I am too weak to move around."

After the first round of drinks, Michael began.

"After you left, a year later I fell in love with a beautiful woman who was my neighbour's daughter. Life was very pleasant, but one day we got the news that some terrorist organization suddenly surfaced in Italy, Spain, Germany and France and started massive aggressive attacks on people, government offices, airports and railway stations. The local police and even the army could not control the situation.

"A small nuclear device was detonated in Paris near the Eiffel Tower, followed by a similar attacks on other European capitals. Several days later London was next, luckily the army was prepared and in about a month most were rounded up. But, these terrorist had spread throughout the country and created havoc bringing the whole country to a standstill. I lost my girl in one of those attacks," He stopped and cleared the tears from his eyes. He waved his glass at Sam, "How about another round, I am thirsty."

While Sam was busy at the bar, David looked at Michael, "Can't believe all this can happen in Europe and Great Britain. Who are these people that have such weaponry and strategy to infiltrate though the defences? They must have accomplices planted in every country."

"Actually it is perhaps our fault. We, in trying to be noble, open our arms in good faith and allow visitors the liberty to come and go under the cover of commerce and tourism. Some came in as refugees from the war torn areas in the Middle East, Africa and Asia, most of them were genuine but a good number were sent by the revolutionaries under that cover with the pretext of escaping the terror of the insurgents."

Sam came back with a tray of glasses, picking one by one and handing them around. Michael began, "I don't think these terrorists had any identification of belonging to any specific area. They had one unique feature that puzzled us."

Michael took a long sip of his Scotch and continued, "On examining their palms, they were blank no finger print or lines. On being questioned they couldn't remember anything, they just showed a number and made a gargling sound as if trying to say something but instead made a vocal clutter. Our prisons are full of them and can't made head or tail of who they are. Most had a small coin size gadget when pressed, an electric discharge produced a hallo like aura around the individual and dissolved his entire body into a muddy puddle.

"As soon as they were captured, they melted themselves, but some were seized and the gadget taken away. Same story in Europe. Until today we don't know who these people are."

Aishtra put in philosophically, "What I think is that these people are very much humans, manipulated by technological advanced people, perhaps…" She stopped. Thinking of Xanthum. She did not want to get into that. It is for Ayond to explain.

"Why did you stop," Michael asked.

"Perhaps it is nothing, you will find a way to handle them." She said and changed the subject, "What is important right now, is to check you out, I'll see if I can help you to get your physical strength back."

"Are you a doctor, I don't think you can do much, what I and many others have gone through during the war, has taken life out of us."

"No I am not a doctor but have some healing tricks, why don't we go to a room and apply those tricks. It might work." She turned around and looked at Sam, "May I have your approval?"

Sam nodded his head in the affirmative, "Do what you can," Then looked at Michael, "She is good, but don't try any funny business, she is my wife."

Aishtra helped Michael up and both disappeared to an adjoining room.

David, Daniel and Sam got up to help themselves at the bar.

She undressed Michael and made him lie down on his stomach with his hands resting on his sides. Aishtra spread her palms fully open and touched him lightly on his shoulder blades bring them down to his buttocks. She did it several times. His body began to glow, pale yellow, and trembled. She held the rare of his ankles and brought her hands sliding up to the back of the knees. Repeated it several times. With her thumb she pressed his spinal cord from below the neck, downwards. He groaned, his body began to glow brighter, changed to a splotch of brightly lit form, and he shivered. She rested both hands on his shoulders, slid them down to his feet, repeated it several times, held his groin firmly, and slapped his buttocks. The light dimmed and began to fade.

She stood and watched. Moments later, Michael moved his hands. Drowsily he murmured, "What happened, had I slept?"

"In a way, actually you had passed out. You will feel some muscular aches that should go away in a few minutes, just remain still."

Aishtra helped him to sit upright. "I feel different, sitting without the hunch." He slid down from the bed and stood upright. He walked a few steps, "I feel like my old self, and can't believe it. You really do have some healing powers."

As they walked back to the room where Sam, Daniel and David were engrossed in conversation. They were amazed to see Michael enter like his old self. "Now throw away that stick, you are a new man," Sam said.

"I slept through the treatment, I have no recollections of what she did," Michael said cheerfully. Sam looked at David and whispered, "The Jinn medicine has worked."

They spent that night at Michael's house.

CHAPTER 10

Jim drove to his old house, parked the car and walked up the front gate. He saw some children playing in the open yard. He walked towards them, they stopped and stared, "Hello, is your father in?" He asked.

A door from the main house opened, "What can I do for you," a man asked.

For a moment no one spoke, Jim recognised his son and walked up to him.

The man came forward and instantly recognised his father. "Hi dad, you look much younger than when you left. Come on in. Children come on and greet your grandfather."

"Why mum is not with you?" is son asked.

"She preferred to stay back, perhaps on a next visit." Jim replies.

They spent hours talking, spoke of the great economic recession and the wars that paralyzed the whole country. "My brother and I moved out of France as life was getting worse there and thought we'll be better off back home, but it was the same. My bother lives alone, not married, I will call him to join us.

Jim told them that he has a few days on Earth and will be returning to Urna with the rest of his friends. He offered if they would like to join him, but they refused. "We are well settled here, after all it is home. We miss you and mother, happy for you, hope to meet both of you on your next visit." One of his sons said.

Jim was told about the atrocities people had faced, "But as long as one does his job and returns home, though monotonous, at least survive the ordeal. Sooner or later, life may return to normal, and we are prepared to take our chances." He was told.

The next day Daniel decided to visit his church and bade farewell to Michael. He told Sam that he would find his way to the church and call for a transport to take him back. There he was greeted by a new face. "Come in Father Daniel, we have heard all about you from Father Scanlon whom you had given the church. He passed away last year and is buried in the courtyard with some of your ancestors, I am Father Shanks."

Daniel noticed a large glass box in a corner near the pulpit, he walked up to it and noticed the artifacts that were hidden away in a room under the Altar. A large photograph of Father Daniel rested at the back of the case.

Father Shanks joined him, "That picture of yours was taken by Father Scanlon on the day you came to say good bye to him before your departure. He told me all about your service to the church and how you found these age old relics. We don't know what they mean but at least they are on display as we consider them part of the church and whoever put them there must have had something to do with the person who built it."

Daniel put his hands to the glass box and bent his head in prayer.

He spent the night in what was his home now occupied by Father Shanks.

Sam, David and Aishtra bade farewell to Michael and decided to visit David's home. Michael's last words were with a bit of humour as they left, "Come again soon, I might need that massage of youth again.

The house where David lived was in a dilapidated state. On the walls outside posters and paint spray in black and red with names and slogans were randomly doodled with obscene drawings and words. Strewn newspapers and food remains scattered on the pathway to the main entrance.

"No decent people can live in such environment, what the world we left behind has turned to be." David said as he avoided carefully the clutter and walked to the door.

He rang the bell and waited. A woman's voice answered from behind the door before opening it. From behind a small gap she said, "What do you want, why don't you people leave us alone. We don't have anything to give you."

She stared at the three of them, perhaps from their dress and looks, she guessed that they were not the regular trouble makers and pest hooligans that had infested the neighbourhood.

David spoke politely, "I used to live here many years ago, just came to check if you are comfortable, we want nothing."

The lady opened the door wide and called, "Dear, we have some guests, you better come out and meet them."

She took them to the room where David had his study, now there were just two chairs and a small table. An old man in his sixties came out wearing a night gown and extended his hand. He shook theirs and apologized for not having enough chairs to sit on.

David introduced himself as the landlord of the house about ten year before and left it to his sons.

"Yes, I remember those young lads, they were very polite and gave us a lot of concessions, when we were unable to pay the rest of the money due to them, they just said, forget it, and the house is yours."

His wife added, "In those days we didn't expect people to be that kind, they were gentlemen from head to toe. It was sad when we heard that both died in action fighting those animal like aggressors who ruined this country."

The news of his sons' death was a thunderbolt that struck David sending him off balance, Sam was quick in holding him and helped him to a chair.

The lady of the house rushed and brought a glass of water and placed it in front of him. "Sorry about the news, I didn't mean to…" Sam interrupted her, "That is alright, the news was a shock to him, he didn't know."

Half an hour later as they were about to leave Sam took an envelope from his pocket and placed it in the man's hand. "There is something for you, I don't need it."

As they left, Aishtra asked Sam "What is in that envelope you gave the man?"

"Some money I got from Michael, he has been holding for me. I don't need it, they can make a good use of it."

CHAPTER 11

They all returned back to the Facility early that evening. Each went to their rooms. Aishtra reported their return to Ayond.

The next day they met at the library. Empty shelves greeted them. "How we had emptied this place was not an easy task. But they are well housed on Urna and have done a lot of good to our generation. They have grown up with a lot of mental affiliation to this planet. Someday, when the people here learn to understand the value of life and be part of a universal society, our people will visit and exchange knowledge." Ayond said.

She told them that while they were away visiting family and friends she had made a few check around the world, where she had placed informers when they lived here, undercover representatives, to report on any unusual activity related to the security of the planet. Unfortunately, most of them were inactive except a few in some remote islands and Australia.

"We have to start all over again, place new informants to keep us update with what is going on. Now tell me, what did you all notice when you made those visits. Anything unusual and what was life like during our absence and the effect of the war in Europe, the Americas and Asia in general."

No one spoke for a while, then Sam broke the silence, "The bad news is that our friend and colleague David has received bad news. His sons while fighting the aggressors were killed in action. It was a blow to all of us, and to David, he lost the only family members he had. We should observe a minute silence in their memory."

Ayond stretched one hand and held Aishtra to her right and the other to David on her left. "We all hold hand and bow our heads in respect."

"I am sorry to hear of your loss David, if you want we can postpone this meeting for some other time."

David shook his head, "No I am alright, let's get on with it. Thank you all for your concern. In you I have a family and I am not alone."

Two attendants entered bringing in tea and coffee. "I think a strong cup of tea is needed." Sam got up to help himself.

The tea break helped to change the atmosphere into informal talk.

"Now to get down to business, tell me Sam how was your trip to Michael, has he anything to say?"

"Michael is alright, but what I have noticed in general of our visits to his place and David's old house, people are not the same, they looked as if they have given up to live, there was some kind of fear I can't explain. Something must have happened to bring them to that state."

Jim interrupted, "Same with my sons, they seemed to live an excluded life style, afraid to trust anyone, perhaps the effect of some kind of calamity that had befallen the nation."

Sam began to narrate what Michael had told them.

"Michael mentioned about a terrorist organization that had massacred millions of people in Europe and elsewhere. The odd thing about them is that they had no finger prints and the palm of their hands are smooth without any lines in them, they had a gadget the size of a coin when pressed the body get electrocuted and dissolve into a puddle like substance," Sam explained.

"I think I know what it is and who those zombies are." Ayond put in, "They are people like you, but physically manipulated to respond to a command from that coin like gadget. On their forehead they have an implant that respond to a command just like robots. Unfortunately the manipulation of their body is irreversible. They are as good as dead. Local terrorists groups who must have entered Europe as refugees some time ago, grouped into gangs and filtered into cities and towns joined hands with local trouble makers. It was easy for the Xanthumians to recruit and change their profile.

"We have seen it elsewhere, and have a way to deal with the situation when the time comes. Let's keep it to ourselves for the time being.

She looked at Daniel, "Anything to repot, how is the church doing?"

"The Brother in charge tells me that only a handful come to pray on Sundays, that also mostly older men and women, people are afraid to come out of their homes, they behave as if they are under a spell."

"That will go away as soon as we disable the satellite the Xanthumians had put up to beam down its hypnotic effect." Ayond explained.

She thought for a while, then added, "I have requested Steve to have the afternoon the day after tomorrow. We shall hear what he has to say about what is really happening to the world and how we can help. I will consult with Argos after our meeting with Steve. Meanwhile I have to collect as much information as possible."

CHAPTER 12

At the far end of the library the team sat at a round table with a large window overlooking the garden. Ayond walked in with Steve and they got up to meet him. "Nice to be with you all," Steve greeted them.

"It is still fresh in our minds the day we said our goodbyes ten years ago, before we left for Urna, and you waving as our ship lifted off." David remembered.

They spent time recollecting the days spent at the facility and their adventure in Egypt to retrieve the device.

Ayond asked Steve to narrate as to what had happened after they last communicated from the ship going to Urna. "Please Steve let's come to the point, tell us what had happened after we left Earth. I remember our last conversation when we were on the spaceship, the reception was bad, and you said something about 'they have done it,'"

"I remember that, what I meant was that they had exploded a nuclear device and there was a response. The Super Powers took sides and the war escalated from the Middle East to Europe. Many countries in the Middle East were reduce to rubble. While this was going on some terrorists smuggled two nuclear bombs into France, one was detonated below the Eiffel Tower and the second on the border with Germany. Some months later, two more bombs were detonated, in southern Russia and South East Asia.

"Then one fine morning some flying saucers were seen hovering over the major cities in Europe, England and the Middle East. They went on a rampage zapping aimlessly at buildings and on people. After a couple of days they stopped and disappeared. Later there was an announcement on TV warning not to assemble in crowds nor carry any weapon, the punishment will be the destruction of the town or the city.

"Every time we went out we looked up if the mysterious big brother was watching. A month later they put up a satellite, we found out that it beamed some kind of waves to affect people's temperament, made them lethargic, weary and docile.

"We knew it all along but kept it from the public, could do nothing to destroy it, fearing a reprisal that would have caused the loss of millions of lives. They had enslaved the whole planet, life had become intolerable, but had to be endured. Luckily they did not bother about our sky gazing facilities, transportation or any of our conveniences and left us to lead our lives normally as long as we behaved. We were afraid to contact you for help, it would have caused more trouble for us. It was only when the asteroid was eliminated we guessed it must have been by you, and bravely made an effort to get in touch. Thanks to Justin, our EW5 head and his team. We were lucky they did not intercept our transmissions, perhaps they underestimated our capabilities." Steve concluded.

Ayond and the rest were in a state of disbelief. Sam was first to speak, "All this happened and none of the Super Powers did anything to stop them."

Steve answered him softly, "If you had been here you would have seen the aliens' might, only one of their saucers would have flattened not only our entire military installations but many cities worldwide."

"I know what you mean, especially after they put up that satellite to control the mind of the populace, there was nothing that anyone could have done. We will take care of that satellite and people will turn to normal. But that will not end your chronic problem, humans love to wage wars. You will see in a few years' time, the same story will begin again. Ayond said and then added.

"With Steve and the government, we should sit and formulate a plan as to how the people of this planet should live in harmony. We had experienced such a situation on our planet some thousands of years ago. A strong leader started the ball to roll, and in a few years brought all faction to the table and made them agree to his terms, threatened them with stringent measures failing their acceptance. In a short time the administration was in full control, achieved its goal, people began to forget animosities and hostile attitudes and were engaged in developing a better future.

"It was easy for us, as we did not have the complexities of the numerous cultures, beliefs, and ethnic groups you are enshrined with. It will not be simple here, but we have to come up with a solution soon, even if the process is going to be ruthless," Ayond said firmly.

"By ruthless, you mean using force," David asked.

"We will go into details after my consultation with my seniors." Ayond replied.

"I think we leave it at that. In the meantime I shall arrange a meeting with Justin's team shortly. Now tell me Ayond, how you keep such a beautiful garden, can I have a look outside," Steve said getting up and walked to the large window.

Ayond pressed a button. A door slid open. They all stepped out. "The light is like sunshine, I was quiet fascinated when I came to visit you the first time ten years ago.

"We are three storeys down, that is artificial light, by our generators," Ayond said.

They all walked up to the far end of the garden, Steve stopped and sniffed at some flowers, Ayond plucked one and buttoned it to his coat's lapel.

After he left they sat at the round table. No one said anything. They were all lost in thought. Aishtra broke the silence. "Why everybody is so morose, the world is ticking outside and where there is life there always can be a better future."

Jim looked at Aishtra and commented softly, "Your words are full of wisdom, humans are very strange species, they are happy in a moment and can be very nasty the next. I don't think anybody can make any change to that. Religions of all kinds are meant to make people live in peace and be worthy human beings, but that has failed and perhaps accelerated the tempo to wage wars."

"Well said Jim but I have something to add here, not all humans are of that nature, there are some who live in peace and don't have that bug in them to be aggressive. It is not religion that makes them so, it is perhaps something in their genes." David began, "The idea may seem ridiculous; once I read an article about the nature of monkeys, to be specific, chimpanzees and another specie called bonobos. The chimpanzees can be aggressive at time and can go on a rampage of violence to kill and plunder. The males rule supreme and the females are down trodden. Have you seen chimpanzees when they are exited they jump around like mad, a trait we inherited to jump up and down when exited, like when watching a football match or when displaying a happy event or conversely. Even some of our dances are an example of that.

"On the other hand the other species known as bonobos are the opposite. They are by nature passive. The females gets preference to eat first, then the left overs are for the males. The males are peace loving and the whole tribe live in harmony.

"What I want to say is that, it is just loud thinking, perhaps the two species have evolved separately to be our ancestors. We have the aggressive nature from one specie and the peace loving from the other."

Aishtra was listening with interest. She could not help, but say something about her kind. "We as Jinn, have both the peaceful and aggressive types. But we did not evolve from monkeys but from smokeless fire as you humans put it. Our creation and evolution is not based on the same principles as humans. David, your observation and conclusion based on what you had read, does have some credence, for humans only," Aishtra looked at Ayond, "What do you think?"

With a smile she said coolly, "What David said makes sense, and that has given me an idea of what we are going to do to tackle our problems. I am not interested as how the human race got their DNA, but we will have to be careful not to treat the entire planet the same way, when we have a solution to implement."

Sam was listening to all what was said and put in very casually, "Here people are of different races, Negroid, Caucasian, Mongoloid and a host of others, they are different in look but under the skin there is no difference.

"As far as I am concerned the true humans are the Negroid. My guess is that the others, or at least some are alien manipulated races." He looked at Ayond, "Forgive me, I don't mean to be cynical. You did mention once that you improved on the human race. However, despite the varied races we are all the same, it is perhaps the cultural upbringing, that each one has a different point of view about, how to greet one another, how to eat, how to worship and so on. These traits are localised, manmade, some are good, and some perhaps with hidden agenda as to how to control your fellow beings for power or financial benefit. These split into more factions again for power, and then you have clashes of these faction roping in many innocent onlookers, resulting in chaos. The world becomes a theater of violence and that is what is happening today."

"I love listening to you all," Ayond said appreciably, "There is enough truth in what you all have said, based on your thoughts it will help me to formulate what action to take, but of course with the approval of our Supreme High. Argos will be our connection between us and him.

"I think we should call it a day. I will contact you as soon as we are ready to meet with Justin and his team.

CHAPTER 13

The day arrived when Justin made all the arrangement to fly to Twin Peaks Island to introduce Ayond and her team to the men and woman who had played an important role in establishing communication with her.

The executive jet landed at the southern tip of the island and a waiting helicopter flew them up to the main observatory. They were greeted by Dr. Frank and his colleagues. At the rest house they spent several hours after the long fourteen hour journey.

They were taken on a tour of the complex. Ayond was fascinated when she stood in a tower at the highest point of the island. On the east, an endless ocean, and its gentle contact with the sandy coastline. The golden hue of the setting sun added to the grandeur of a picturesque view. On the east, the boisterous waves lashed mercilessly at the countless strewn boulders and rocks that littered its precipitous coast line.

"A solitary but peaceful environment. I could sit for hours admiring the landscape." Ayond.

"From here our security personnel keep a watch at uninvited guests." Dr. Frank said as they stepped down and walked up to the observatory.

"We have instruments and computers no other observatories or nations have. The state of the art, to monitor space activity, and have devises direct or neutralise any vehicles or probes in flight. The best brains on Earth had contributed in what is here." Dr. Frank proudly explained. "It was from here that we saw the approach of the giant asteroid, we were certain that it will hit Earth and end all life and turn this planet into a pile of an inferno.

"When we saw it shatter to bits, it was not long before we guessed that you had something to do with its demise. Thanks to Steve's help to contact you."

Ayond responded, "Earth has been our home going back thousands of years. We have probes all over the solar system, constantly vigilant. We saw it coming much before you did, far beyond the Kuiper Belt. We then began preparation to deal with it. A space ship similar to the one we came in, but have more deadly weaponry that can shatter your moon into bits, with that power an asteroid could be disintegrated with just one zaps.

"It was our Supreme High who suggested that we visit Earth and tell you all about it and he also said that any other form of danger threatening the existence of your world, whether natural or otherwise, should be handled accordingly.

"Though he is not a living being, yet he has an affiliation to this world, he too lived here for a long time, much before humans became a social entity. He explicitly said and I quote, 'tell the humans, had it not been for us, they would have been a pile of ash. We have given them a new lease on life and have rightfully inherited their guardianship and as custodians, will show them the way to enjoy a happy life.' Those words gave us the green light to perform as would deem fit.

"As we are all here let me tell you what we have found, that was eroding the human race to bring them to a vegetated state. You as scientists perhaps knew that something was wrong but left you guessing or afraid to come out with a solution. Soon we will disable that satellite that is beaming down waves affecting the mental state of the populace. After a short while the effect would wear off.

"Our suspicion arose when on our way to Earth spotted space ships of an evil race that was stealing your gold. We had to destroy them, and without being detected by you, sent some of our crafts discretely and destroyed their bases and mining operations.

"This evil race is known to us since we first came Earth about fifteen thousand years ago. We then fought them and warned them that if they ever returned they would be dealt with harshly. They live on one of Jupiter's moons, originally they come from a dying planet in the Cygnus constellation. They are what you might call a reptilian race. They are known as Xanthumains; Xanthum was their lord and master. His subsequent successors inherited that title and traits from time immemorial.

"Anyhow, nothing to worry about, so long as we are here. When we return to Urna, we will deal with them once and for all."

Walking around leisurely within the observatory Ayond commented, "I am quite impressed by what you have here. Once we set things right, we will vitalise and share our sciences and technologies and open doors of knowledge that you cannot comprehend."

On the fourth day the visitors to Twin Peaks Island left. Back in London, Steve and Justin decided to sit and recap what Ayond had mentioned, "I wonder what she meant by being our guardians. She kept talking about the Supreme High as a person who has the final word. Tell me more about him," Justin asked.

"I may have talked about him earlier but no harm in repeating. I had met him. You will be surprised if I told you that he is a highly sophisticated computer. I would confidently say he is the ultimate machine, he can do anything even control the movement of their planet, or destroy it, if he wishes. He is like a God to them, and he expects to be respected like one. They have a miniature size computer called Argos, made by the Supreme High which can communicate with his maker while they are here on Earth.

"She also mentioned about revitalising life and make us happy. To be honest, I did not understand what she meant, perhaps to share knowledge and boost our understanding of things. We will perhaps develop into a super race."

"Imagine that little planet of theirs, they are so advanced," Justin commented.

"They are hundreds of thousand years ahead of us, and they have the Supreme High, their God as far as I am concerned," Steve elucidated.

"God or a computer who cares, as far as he can deliver and look after his people in the real sense of the word, he is not a hypothetical Deity," Justin said and got up, "Ayond is going to call you in a few days, we should meet at the EW5 headquarters and will provide her with all our data and personnel. From her talk, I foresee a difficult task ahead of us."

CHAPTER 14

Almost a week and no news from Ayond. Sam and the rest of the team took liberties to go out and spend most of their time visiting restaurants and old friends. The general atmosphere outside presented a sorry state. People in general looked morose. At bars and restaurants people were less vocal, just drank, ate and went home in a wobbly state.

With that pathetic state the environment offered, they decided to stay in and make the best use the facility could offer. The gym and the cafeteria were always an option. They played music and dragged some of the staff to the dance floor.

Finally the day arrived when Ayond accompanied by her team arrived at Justin's office. She was told that the Prime Minister would be joining them.

Ayond sat with Aishtra, Sam and Jim to her left, David and Daniel to her right. On the opposite side of the table Steve and Justin with an empty chair in between.

The door opened and the Prime Minister dressed casually entered, "Hello everybody," he said and gabbed a chair.

"No Sir, this is your chair," Justin got up and pointed to the chair between him and Steve.

"Thank you Justin," as he sat down he looked at the team sitting opposite him. "It is a pleasure meeting you again, before we start I want to make a request, please address me by my first name. To all my friends I am Bill. We must do away with all the formalities."

"Very well," Steve began, "We can talk freely and express our views openly as this meeting is very important to decide our future plans as to how we can make this planet of ours liveable without the threat of wars and acts of terror.

"Bill, before we begin, I want to introduce to you a very special person in Ayond's team, Mrs. Aishtra, though she is from Earth but not human.

"Not human and from this Earth, what do you mean," Bill looked puzzled and stared at her.

"Yes Bill, she belongs to a specie known as Jinn, I don't recollect mentioning her to you earlier." Then he went on to explain what a Jinn is.

"Do we have them on the British Isles too?" Bill asked and looked at Justin.

"Everywhere on Earth, just as I said they look like us, the only difference is their eyes, their pupil is not round but elongated, like in felines. They also have the ability to change their form to any shape they wish to be."

Bill got up from his chair, "Forgive me lady, but can I have a look at your eyes."

He walked to the other side and Aishtra stood up. He came close to her, "They look better than ours." He shook her hand and went back to his seat.

"Now you have introduced everyone to me, I'll say a few words about myself. I come from a humble background. My father and grandfather were school teachers. Because of them I had the fortune to read a lot of books, you just name it and we had it in our house, and I read them all. Got into politics through encouragement from some colleagues of mine and here I am at thirty five, became Prime Minister with a landslide majority." He thanked Steve and added, "The floor is open for our meeting, let's begin."

Justin looked at him, "Steve, anything you want to add."

"Nothing much to say for the moment, but I personally wish to thank Ayond and her team for coming all the way to check on us at a time we most need them. What Ayond has in mind might seem undesirable from our point of view but with the guidance of the all-knowing Supreme High, might just be the answer to our problems."

There was a few moments of silence, then Ayond started.

"Thank you Steve," she looked at Bill and Justin, "I will come to the point, the situation in your world is not simple. You had the greedy and selfish Xanthumains, but that threat will no longer exist after we deal with them on our return to Urna.

"Your problem is with your people. They have gone astray, power hungry and the few who have accumulated untold wealth at the cost of their country's well-being, sad to say, have influenced some of the your super powers," she looked at Bill, "Sorry for being so impertinent and you know what I mean. During the few days since we arrived I have obtained a full report on who are responsible for the mess you are in.

"The Middle East is in ruins, beautiful cities reduced to rubble, looking like battle fields. There are a handful of culprits assisted by a few, who channel massive amounts of money to create wars and economic anarchy, all for their personal interest. This must be uprooted at any cost. It is like a bad tree, no use to trim off or cut the branches, if it is troubling you, cut it off from its roots. This will also apply to other regions of the world where they have bitter relations with neighbors.

"Secondly you have the Super Powers, they are equally at fault in many ways. They favour nations where they have economic or strategic interest. Those nations can commit and finance crime on an international scale, and they know it, but give a blind eye, again with due respect, you know what I mean," Ayond looked at Bill.

"Thirdly you have the hooligans and terrorists who bully the common man on the street. Very little is done to eliminate them. In some ways they are connected to that malicious tree.

"My fourth point is, you have puppet regimes, supported and funded by illegitimate sources.

"Finally, I can easily include the misuse and abuse of religion by some dictators or the upholders of the faith; to justify their authority and spread their sphere of influence on unsuspecting innocent people and poor nations to sing their song whenever they demand it. That must be stopped. I will not elaborate more on this. You and many more are not familiar with their mental set up. It is deep rooted within and has become the order of the day. Like an undetectable virus.

"Let me add one point, there are many cultures, very few really understand their inner traits, they judge one another by their own, and try to impose it on the unsuspecting and the innocent. It is difficult for the western mind to comprehend what I am saying. Don't judge them by your own, it would be unfair. Only reasoning may bring about a suitable solution. In the absence of that, brings in commotion and the clash of cultures. Worth giving it a serious thought."

Ayond paused, looked at the attentive gentlemen sitting in front of her.

There was a knock on the door and a young female entered. Justin made a sign to come in. She asked him as to when to have a tea break.

"You are on time," he looked around, "How about it?"

They all nodded and someone said, "A strong cup of tea is needed."

During the break, no one talked about what transpired in the meeting, they talked in general of how people passed their time on Urna.

Back again to the meeting. Bill started, "Ayond I must congratulate you on your observations and you have hit the nail on the head on all points. And, if I may ask, how we are going to correct it, is easily said than done."

"True Bill, honestly speaking, some governments are run by corrupt people who have no feeling for the common man. Sorry to say, even some of the Super Powers have that bug. To bring a change requires a lot of courage and sacrifice.

"Let me tell you about our planet. It is one large continent and one ethnic populace. Quite different from your set up. Nevertheless, some thousands of years ago we experienced similar situations you are facing now. Animosities and wars. But then we were blessed with an honest leader who influenced some elders and in a short time brought about a change, how to live in harmony and concentrate on technological development and do away with poverty and disease.

"At first it was not easy, we had the bad guys who opposed such governance. From our archives I studied in detail how they brought about this revolutionary change in a matter of a few years. With an iron hand they put the fear of God to achieving it; using your expression. After some time, we attained a life that could not be happier. We are now part of your solar system; we want to make sure not to have noisy neighbours.

"With your numerous cultures and beliefs, would be difficult to accomplish this at first, but in my deliberation at the world body of nations, which I am planning to do, will make them an offer they cannot refuse.

"An example from your world. Turkey for instance. Prior to Kamal Ata Turk, the country was known to be called the sick man of Asia. Primitive, archaic in every way. In a short time Kamal turned it to a model of a nation. It was courage and foresight.

"No doubt, for some time there will be opposition and turmoil, sadly many lives may suffer, but after one or two generations it would become the accepted way of life. A sacrifice for the benefit of mankind.

"The virus ten years ago, brought down your world population to half. People are still recouping, mostly in South and Easter Asia. For the time being we will not include them in our plans, show some leniency, but will surely have to come under the fold in due course. It is the Middle East, Africa, Europe and to some extent the Americas, will bear the brunt of our strategies.

"Because of the madness of wars that was brewing worldwide ten years ago, we decided to leave Earth, which was our home for thousands of years, as it was not our policy to interfere with your squabbles, we left you to solve your problems and you have failed.

"Now is the time for us to act. Why so? Having saved you from total extinction from an asteroid, we gave you a new lease to continue living, at the same time, rightfully earned us the title to be your guardians in a strict sense. We love that you continue to rise and shine strictly on our terms and it is not negotiable. Now I would request you all to think about what I have said, want an input from each one of you, and what our line of action should be, which of course should be acceptable to us," Ayond concluded.

David adjusted himself on his chair and leaned forward.

"This reminds me of reading in a book about a traveller in the early 19th century in what you call the Levant. He said after a lot of deliberations that people there always have quarrels and the best way to maintain peace is and I quote, 'strike terror and inspire respect'.

"That was a crude way of putting it, but that must have been the order of the day in those days. Perhaps a new form of world governess to maintain sanity among people where all nations would live in harmony and give up their squeamish behaviour, though it is a farfetched idea.

"A watchful eye to monitor the activities of nations, rules to be implemented based on their economic status, social set up and beliefs, strictly to be obeyed. Any deviation from the set rules laid would be punishable by extreme measures. It would be hard in the beginning but as time goes by old habits fade away. In the past, Europe or the western world in general corrected itself through strict laws and education.

"In the past the high handed religious orders in Europe retarded the progress of science and technology. A good example of progress, is the United States of America. A new nation established little less than three hundred years ago has grown to be the most powerful country in the world. While others who boast of thousand years of culture are far behind."

"Well said David, I fully understand what you are getting into. Anyone else?" Ayond asked. "How about you Daniel?"

He was prompt, "I was a parish priest in my days on Earth, and you know what it is like to be so, but since I have joined your team and my stay on Urna, have reformed my concept of religion and how I view it now. The theatrical dress we wear or the fancy ornamentations, the chanting or the verbal display of words to impress upon the poor and ignorant masses, all those acts were artificial and misrepresentations.

"Not only have we, but nearly all religions have symbols in stones, paintings or the like that represent God. What I have found on Urna during my stay there, watched people, they had no places of worship. One of the wise men whom I spent many hours picking his brain, told me that his place of worship is in his mind. On Earth we would say, in one's heart. He explained that in the days of ignorance many thousand years ago, they carried small figurines on their person as a good luck charm, to protect them from evil. In due course, they began to worship them. This gradually turned into a cult giving way to the growth of many other cults, became a fashion, and led to political ideas, which ultimately brought the downfall of rational reasoning and the start of an age of ignorance.

"In a nut shell, it brought about chaos; strong and forward thinking individuals brought about changes, cruelly carried out with success, and the result is what they are now, blessed with eternal joy. I have become a believer in that conviction.

"One more thing I want to add, all religions are good, so long as people understand their true purpose. But not when they deviate for personal gains and use it as a weapon to control. It is done all over, with some exceptions." Daniel concluded.

There was a few moments of silence then Sam spoke. "Very well said Daniel, I am impressed, you have become a true believer without the displays of antiquated ceremonies. Ayond, you might like to make a note of what the learned Daniel has said."

"Can't imagine what I have heard in this meeting, looks like we are heading for a *new world order*. Hard to conceive it's coming to fruition, in my personal view. As a Prime Minister, I wish you all the luck. Ayond, if I may ask you, how you are going to deliver your message to the world. You will have a lot of obstacles, not from me but from other world leaders," Bill put in gently.

"I will prepare a speech to read out at the United Nations. Before that, I will discuss my plans in one week's time. Once we all agree, we will proceed from there." Ayond said.

CHAPTER 15

During the week Steve and Justin met privately at the EW5 office. Justin murmured but audible, "Ayond plans to reshape our ancestral heritage way of life. That is a tall order if you know what I mean."

"Let us not jump to conclusion, there are many issues involved here," Steve began, "Take the Middle East for an instance. Their troubles are very complex. Same religion but with many variations in beliefs. There was a time nobody bothered what sect believed in what, at least not as blatantly as it is today. We are aware of the source of all this and the purpose behind it. Since those responsible have become filthy rich overnight because of the untold quantity of natural resources which the rest of the world thrive on, they have become untouchable and the world hypocritically gives a blind eye to their transgressions.

"Their operations are so secretive that the majority of the world do not suspect them. They have created divisions among people, as a result wars are being fought to this day. In other parts of the world governments are at logger heads with one another, it is in our nature, perhaps it is in our diet that makes it so. I just hope that when the world is reminded about the asteroid, sanity will prevail, and accept the goodwill of the aliens. But knowing some of the high and mighty, brand the idea as a conspiracy, a plot to rule the world."

"Steve, are we speculating, here we are dealing with world politics, not in world's welfare. The Super Powers can unite with the aliens as a team and work out a middle path where all nations would agree to rule independently, but under one flag, like the United States of America; a United States of the World. No doubt there will be many oppositions but if Ayond plays her cards well, we might achieve it, and I can palpably tell you, not even that will come without a struggle." Justin observed.

Steve and Justin continued their discussion and decided to go along with whatever Ayond would suggest, "She is a well-wisher and means well, just imagine a world with no wars, no terrorist attacks, time and money would be spent on the development technology, medicine and get rid of poverty. What a great world it will be." Steve envisioned.

"What about Russia and China, will they accept this change. Doubtful, both are old and well established nations, their traditions go a long way. If they join in must have a say in governance of the new order with a tinge of their colours. If you have studied the emergence of most religions for instance, they began by incorporating discretely some of the old 'beliefs' within for the new faith to be acceptable."

"Goes without saying Justin, their contribution will have an added virtue. The main thing is to get them to the conference table," Steve added.

Justin thought for a while then began philosophically, "Once this is over, I want to sit with Ayond and ask her openly as to what exactly they have contributed to the human race during their fifteen thousand years stay on Earth. Were there other visitors before them beside the evil Xanthum and what were their contribution?"

"You missed out one prime question, did they or some others influenced in the concept and development of religions and beliefs, and did they play around with our genetics." Steve added.

"That would be interesting, I do have a hypothesis on what you have said, I am sure she will tell us the truth and prove my point, at least privately." Justin said and added, "It is a delicate subject but worth a try. I am very comfortable with your views and thinking, our minds think alike and I hope Ayond's associates, the Earth team wouldn't cause a problem."

"On the contrary, they are a very gentle lot, met them before they left with Ayond, they will be an asset." Steve added.

Moments later Justin began, almost talking to himself with a cynical expression, "Getting back to what Ayond and her Supreme High have in store for us, perhaps take over the planet and run it using force and turn us into some kind of freaks, clinically tuned to obey orders."

"You are jumping to conclusions unnecessary, they are not that unreasonable, and after all they had lived on Earth for so long. If they had the intention, would have done it so easily at that time. Besides, she said that she would consult us and have our approval before going into action. We had the Xanthumian guys manipulating the human race without us realizing it. They were stealing our gold. Thanks to Ayond to get rid of them. We have to be careful, their way of life may be good on their planet, it may not be workable here, but do we have a choice?"

"I agree, let's wait and see what her ideas are. You will support me if there is any conflict of views." Justin added.

"Goes without saying Justin, let us leave it at that. By the way, I am quite impressed by Bill. Being a Prime Minister at such a young age he is so down to earth. Good upbringing, out of a literate lineage not an upstart. He will go a long way."

"Surely, he will contribute wisely to what has to be said in our meeting with Ayond."

They were interrupted by a buzz on the telephone. "The Prime Minister is on the line."

"Hello Justin, I was looking for Steve and I am told he is with you."

"Yes Bill, you have a long life as they say, we were just talking about you."

"Great minds think alike, I felt that we have not talked in so many days, wanted to hear from both of you. Nothing important, just want to chit chat. Can I come over and join you."

"You are most welcome."

"Will be with you in about half an hour."

Justin put the phone down and looked at Steve, "Let's pick his brains a bit and hear what he has in mind."

Bill's entrance was rather sporty, he flung the door open and, "Here I am gentlemen, five minutes late but made it. Behind him walked in a gorgeous looking female in her early thirties, "This is my confidential secretary Fiona, I brought her along, and she will be involved in taking notes of all that goes on in our meeting with the alien Ayond. She will keep all records, strictly confidential."

Both Steve and Justin got up to meet them. Justin slipped out of the door and asked his secretary to get some tea.

After an exchange of some niceties over tea, Fiona got up and collected the empty cups and put them aside on an adjoining table.

"Well," Bill began, "What have you been talking about, you two."

"In general, about how the alien lady Ayond and her team are going to put things in shape to influence the whole of mankind to change for the better. We see a difficult situation in achieving that goal. Humans are difficult to change, for good or bad. Take the example of religion, whenever a new one comes, it comes to stay through violence and bloodshed.

"Wars are fought for territorial or economic gains. It is in our nature, you have seen recently people of the same faith and culture are killing each other, prompted by hidden hands and agendas, of the same faith and culture. In some other parts of the world terrorism has become another issue. Some leaders, in our opinion, encourage the big powers to do their dirty work when they don't like the face of a leader. How can a new order come to fruition to make a Utopia of life on this beautiful planet? We, as humans may look the same, but predominantly split into countless strictly different cultures and beliefs, as if each one is a different species. Can we achieve that change?"

Bill listened attentively to Justin while doodling on a piece of paper. He jotted one word in bold capital letters, 'NEVER' and he picked it up and faced it to Steve and Justin.

"That is what we thought also, but we must keep in mind what she clearly mentioned about them having rightfully inherited the guardianship of this world after saving us from the asteroid threat." Justin remarked.

"That gave them the right to do as they pleased, like if you inherit an old depleted house, you would improve on it and make it better to live in. Their concept is same for trying to make our home a better place to live in." Steve added philosophically.

The conversation carried on for an hour spilling their thoughts openly. Then there was a few moments of silence.

"Excuse me sir, may I have a word," Fiona interjected.

"Go ahead, we love to listen to what you have to say." Bill replied.

"I am an outsider, only now I am listening to what you all had to say. This alien friend seem to care about us humans, otherwise why she would come all the way to help us. As I understand from the notes I have read, their big boss has acquired a Utopian world for his people, they are happy and have achieved a sense of brotherhood. We should listen to her attentively and give her a chance to say what she has to say, she may feel the same way as you all do."

Bill was pleased by what Fiona had to say, "From your first attendance to our meeting you seem to have grasped the situation well. I am quite impressed, Steve what do you think about including her in all our meetings, not as a secretary, but a member of our team."

"I agree, how about you Justin?"

"She will be an asset, why not," Justin put in.

"Well it is settled, congratulations Fiona. As for now we will wait for Ayond to contact us. Keep me informed of any thoughts you all might have," he looked at Fiona and added, "You too Fiona.

CHAPTER 16

The day arrived when Ayond and her team assembled at Justin's office, Bill's arrival was monumental as he stepped in accompanied by Fiona. They all got up from their seats and stared at the model of a figure, the beauty that accompanied him.

The men rushed to introduce themselves and shook hands. Bill began softly, "This is Fiona, my confidential secretary and with your permission I would like to involve her in our discussions. You will find her most useful."

Ayond looked at her focussing her thoughts into her mind. She looked at Bill and teasingly commented briefly. "Bill, I like your taste," then she looked at Fiona, "You are most welcome, a friend of Bill is a friend of ours."

On one side of the table Ayond sat with her team and on the opposite side Bill and his.

"Steve you must have briefed Fiona about our background," Ayond asked.

"Yes she read most of the files."

"Well, let us begin. I will introduce my team for the sake of Fiona. On my right is Aishtra, next to her is Sam her husband, on my left is David, Jim and Daniel. With the consent of my colleagues here, and authorized by the instructions of our Supreme High, I can take any action as I please. I thought of consulting some world leaders of unbiased decisions, sadly, I found none to qualify.

"I am not going to elaborate on that, it does not concern us here at the moment. But will value the opinion of my old friend Steve, and of course, Bill and Justin.

"The earth people are too deeply entrenched in their old ways. Difficult to change for the better. Here I am referring to the old world, east of the Americas. On the other hand, the nations of North America have emerged with a new democratic experiment, the United States and Canada.

"You have witnessed what people can do. Immigrants from the old world made a new way of life for themselves. Without the ambiguity of old thinking they embarked on a new order to live in harmony. Though there were obstructions and wars, but soon they emerged as an exemplary advanced nations. One example, a United Fifty States as one, why not a World States as one. Will it not be a dream to have a peaceful family living under one roof?

"As far as the old world, Russia and China can contribute much more, provided their so called way to rule is revised and incorporated within. They can contribute unlimited knowledge, thousands of years of traditions, if focused correctly, can bring wonders.

"Think about what I have said. It is a tall order but worth a try. As far as the warring factions, wherever they are, we will handle them our way. First we thought of targeting some areas, but in the process it would bring suffering to the innocent. We will work out a way to deal with those bad elements.

"Bill, I request you not to indulge in discussing what we have talked in this room with other leaders, it will be premature."

"Mum is the word," Bill said putting his hand to his mouth.

Ayond looked at Fiona and Bill and made a request. "I would like Fiona to be part of my team if you have no objection to that."

Bill looked at Fiona, "I have no objection if she is willing. She will initially have to perform some duties with me, you have to let her go for some time, and then she is all yours. What do you say Fiona?"

Fiona was at a loss to answer immediately as it had happened so sudden. She looked at Ayond, "How can I be of any help, know nothing of your ways, I am a simple office secretary."

"I have special plans for you, if you agree. When you are ready come along with Bill and Steve to our premises and stay behind after they leave, I will personally see to your comfort."

She agreed.

Before they left Fiona walked up to Aishtra, "I am amazed by what I read about you. Just want to look at your eyes," Staring hard for several moments, "The rest of you is like us I presume."

"Very much like you," Aishtra replied with a smile.

CHAPTER 17

Bill, Justin, Steve and Fiona arrived three days later at the alien's residential Facility and were taken to the library where Ayond and her team had assembled.

"After a few exchanges of niceties, Ayond began. "My plan is not to be conspicuous in the war torn countries where no reason works. Let us play a little game, a supernatural performance with a discrete warning. Being believers in superstitions and anecdotes from past historical events, a scenario of that kind would be displayed with a hint that wars must end and people must live in harmony and peace, or else misfortune would fall upon those who do not comply. Initially we would be gentle and accommodating, a few '*heavenly displays*' might do the trick. But living in the twenty first century such displays may back fire; but we will give it a try anyhow. If they ignore our warnings we will display some of our powers without harming anyone."

Steve raised his hand and interrupted, "They will not fall for that, they are thick skinned and will blame the super powers. It has to be something dramatic."

"I am coming to that, Aishtra would use her Jinn skills in disguising as a tall old man walking on the streets calling for peace, and if the warnings go unheeded, some punishment would fall upon the people.

"Fiona, you would appear as a hologram flying aimlessly all over, then merge with a dark formation of clouds that we will administer with some flashes through the angry clouds followed by monstrous blasts of bolts of lightning they had not seen before. Aishtra will also take part in that.

"We will start from the Western Sahara desert, right across to the Middle East and beyond as far as Myanmar. It is humanly impossible to perform what I plan to do, they will have to believe that it is a message ordained. Out of fear they have to submit," She paused and added, "Hopefully. We will give it a try.

"As I was saying, Aishtra and Fiona's demonstrations will last several days, in addition the dark clouds would be injected with harmless chemicals to descend upon buildings and people, which would have a foul smell, like rotten eggs.

"Aishtra as an old man will continue her visits to different locations, counselling people to live in peace, stop all wars otherwise face a punishments ordained. We will use one of our small ships in its invisible form. Let's hope it will bring some sense into their thick heads."

"I doubt if it will work. In this day and age, people are familiar with such technological spectacles and will certainly blame it on the West. Hollywood films have shown such acrobatics and the whole exercise will fall flat," David observed.

"I agree with you David, I will work it out in such a way that the whole act will look natural. Perhaps we should begin our act with an unprecedented gigantic dust storm for several days, followed by heavy rain accompanied by winds exceeding two hundred miles per hour. It is worth a try, then they may fall for it. No harm in trying. The technology we are capable of is beyond any on Earth, even your Hollywood. After it is all over we will study the after effects and act accordingly." Ayond put in.

Sam thoughtfully commented, "Once it is done successfully, all countries will be brought together to the United Nations to meet an alien from another world, it would make it very obvious for the warring factions to deduce that the dramatic display was the work of the aliens. The whole exercise would be deemed a failure."

"Not quite so, Sam. At least we would have brought them to the conference table and if they think we were behind those displays, all the better, they would know of our capabilities and strength. I am going to tell the world of our serious intentions to bring order in a peaceful manner. No nonsense bargaining would be tolerated, it will be 'take it or leave it and face the consequences.' And of course to remind them that we are the guardians." Ayond got up and led her guests on a tour of the Facility and showed them Argos, the Supreme High's miniature representative.

Justin turned to Ayond with a humorous note, "Please keep Argos happy, we don't want him displeased in anyway."

Ayond assured Bill that Fiona will be safe with her and not to worry. "You can accompany us when we begin our show of fireworks."

After the grand tour, they left. Fiona was accommodated in a room next to the rest of the team.

The following day they met in David's room, "Just like the good old days when we were first brought out here in search of the Medallion.

They filled Fiona with every detail and in turn Fiona asked questions about life on Urna.

Daniel took the lead, "It is a world with people like us, strange phenomena, but the universe is so large, nothing is impossible, after all life must have started from the original dust the universe was made of.

"When we first arrived they were fascinated by us, their government had introduced the English language and they were quick to learn. Their form of worship looked strange to me, but in due course understood its meaning. It is a kind of philosophy, no entity to worship, or a building filled with statues, they just have a simple idea, 'to be good and to be better."

Fiona was listening attentively when someone shouted, "Anyone for a drink?"

They all raised their hand, Aishtra and Sam did the honours.

"Tell me Daniel, you were a parish priest before you left, what made you change?" Fiona asked.

"No I have not changed, in a way still continue to be the same, but not as I was before. Here we actually worship stones that symbolize God, in the form of buildings or statues, even paintings. Traditions have made us so, something to feel and touch. But actually, an individual should have it all this in his heart and mind"

Sam came in with the drinks, "Daniel stop your preaching, talk about the good life out there. May be Fiona will be interested to join us when we leave."

"No thank you, I prefer to stay here."

"Tell me Daniel, are you married?" Fiona asked directly.

"No, I never gave it a thought."

Joined by Sam, the three chatted until little later dinner was served.

CHAPTER 18

The next day no news from Ayond.

The team had one additional person, Fiona. They were quite fascinated by her general knowledge and special interest in human behaviour. They talked about the days prior to their meeting with Ayond.

"The way life was in our days on Earth, a routine living, same thing day after day. Now we are involved in correcting the behaviour of the human race that has gone haywire." David was in conversation with Jim and Daniel.

"Living on Urna we quickly adapted their life style, because there was no pressure from anyone how to behave or dress or conduct ourselves. They live easy, do as they please, they are happy and make others happy. Freedom of thought without any strings attached. It is perhaps a typical state of Utopia! Of course their Supreme High is watching all the time. The word violence does not exist, it does not make them less 'manly.'"

"You are correct in saying all these good things about them," Jim interjected, "But doesn't life become monotonous without occasional quibbles."

"I see the Earthly trait still in you Jim, it does not matter, will wear off in due course."

Daniel put it gently. "As far as I am concerned," he continued, "In my previous life as a parish priest here on Earth, yes I consider this life like rising from the dead, to a better one on Urna, in a world hundreds of thousands of years older in terms of knowledge and technological achievements. This is like being in a divine place, no wars, no pestilence, food is plenty and on top of that live in harmony." He paused and his listeners waited if there was more wisdom coming from him.

"It will be a long time before humans can achieve that goal. So long as we are divided into races, racism shall rule in all its forms. Not only by the colour of our skin or what we look like, but within that racial multifaceted category there exists a racial superiority in many forms, or whatever you may call it.

"Look at their Supreme High for instance, they know he is there and depend on him in good times and bad times. He acts. In our world we have a Supreme High whom we call god, but in many forms, in different lands. To all of us He is the All Mighty, the same entity, but each one looks at Him with different coloured glasses. When we are in trouble and need help, our calls go on deaf ears. It only means one thing, and I leave to you, to think deeply. Wars, envy and hatred will always rule on Earth." Daniel stopped and gave a deep sigh. He was emotionally exhausted.

"There is a lot of sense in what you said, but it is wrong to pass judgement on the belief of billions. May be He is watching how we behave and when the appropriate time comes He will act. Read your history, there have been several examples when He showed His anger. It is wrong to pass judgement randomly. To change the subject, I wonder what Ayond is up to and how she is going to handle the situation we are in." David concluded.

Fiona sat alone in the garden in deep contemplation. Sam sat in a corner of the room reading a book.

Aishtra came in with a message from Ayond. "You would not believe this, she is floating somewhere over Brazil just now, has been visiting every corner of the globe assessing situations and how to deal with them. She has asked me to tell you to feel free to visit outside, but be back by Sunday, six days from now."

With that message all started making preparations to visit friends or relatives.

"Perhaps it is going to be our last, so let us make the best of it." Sam said.

Sam, David and Aishtra got into one car, Jim decided to visit his sons.
"What about you Daniel," Sam asked.

"I would rather stay, I have nowhere to go."

Fiona interrupted, "Why not you and I go and visit my family and friends. A bit of an outing will do us good, how about it Daniel?"

Daniel thought for a moment and agreed to go.

Sam drove to Michael's place. The house was bubbling with the sound of music. "He will not hear the doorbell with that racket," someone said. But then the door opened. Michael greeted them with open arms and ushered them in.

"You couldn't have come at a better time. I am having some friend."

The room was full with men and women, some were chatting and a few were dancing. Michael had to go and stop the music and with a loud voice announced their arrival. "Ladies and gentlemen, let me introduce you to my cousin Sam, his wife Aishtra and my friend David. They are the ones I had talked about, who chose a better life somewhere in the cosmos, on a planet called Urna. You can pick their brains and find out more. The lady will stay with me to ask her for some advice." He held Aishtra by the hand and led her to a corner of the room where they sat down.

"Sam, feel at home and serve your friend and me with some refreshments, you know where the bar is."

The party went on, some surrounded David and heard stories that engrossed his listeners while Sam did the same with the women.

Aishtra asked Michael about his health. "Can't you see, I am completely recovered, as good as new, perhaps one more treatment by your healing hands before you go."

"Glad to, Michael, this time I will make you feel as good as a young man of thirty. If we ever visit Earth again you will still look as young as ever. You will hardly change in many years. When your guests leave I will give you the treatment again, but this time you must rest completely on the bed for twenty four hours. No food or any activity."

It was near midnight that the final guest left. Sam, David and Aishtra sat informally. Aishtra got up and took Michael away. "Sam," She called, "I am taking Michael for treatment, he must not be disturbed in any way, so say your good byes and must leave him alone after I finish with him."

The two disappeared into the bedroom and made him lie face down on the bed with his shirt and pants removed.

"Shut your eyes, put your hands straight on your sides and don't move."

Michael obediently followed her instructions.

Aishtra being a Jinn began to take a new form. Her body began to glow, dimly at first, then grew stronger, her luminous hands moved over his back not touching. With her thumb caressed his spinal cord from bellow his neck downwards. Michael's body shivered. She repeated the same several times until there was a groan from Michael. With both palms touched his shoulder blades and gently pressed taking them down to his buttocks. His entire body began to light up with a bluish aura.

With each palm pressed his thighs moving downward stopping at the back of his knees, she gripped them hard and held them for a few second. Michael jerked with a whimper. She slid her palms down to his calves, touching gently and stopped at the ankles, pressed hard with her thumb and index finger. Michael once again let out a moan.

Her palms began to glow brighter and with several sweeping movements across his entire body she rested them at the bottom of his head. The glow on her body began to fade away.

The blue halo around Michael's body continued to glow, she waited until it too faded away.

"Can you hear me Michael?" she asked.

There was a very faint yes from him. She struggled to dress him up and turned him on his back. Saw to his comfortable posture she softly whispered in his ear, "You must not get up, go to sleep and tomorrow afternoon get out of bed gently and have your lunch. You might feel dizzy but it will wear off soon. We will see ourselves out, you have our telephone number, call us if you need anything."

"How is he taking it," Sam asked.

"He is as good as new," Aishtra said.

They spent the night at Michael's and left the next day.

Fiona and Daniel drove leisurely through a small village and stopped near a park. "Come on Daniel, this park is very special to me, I grew up in the neighbourhood and every evening my parents and I used to come here for a stroll. There is a bench somewhere here where I carved my name. Let me show it to you."

She playfully ran and stood near a bench. "Here it is, you can see my name on the back rest, and it says 'Fiona.'"

Daniel touched her engraved name, "So this is where you used to sit?"

"Yes, actually my father donated that bench and I for fun decided to engrave my name."

"You must have been a mischievous girl."

"Our house is just across from where I parked the car. Let's go and meet my parents."

Her father answered the door and let them in. Her mother was playing the piano with her back towards the door and didn't hear them come in. Fiona stealthily walked up to her and put her palms on her eyes.

"Stop it whoever you are," She touched the hands gently, 'Hold it, these are familiar, is it you Fiona up to your tricks."

She introduced Daniel and sometime during a conversation Fiona's mother put a blunt question. "Where did you get that gorgeous looking man, you have always been a choosy one. I am so happy for you, when is the big day."

"Mother, stop it. There is no big day we are just friends, work together in an office."

"You always talk of work, it is about time to start living like other girls of your age," she stopped and looked at Daniel, "Sorry young man, I didn't get your name." Promptly he replied, "Daniel."

To stop him from going into his parish past, Fiona completed the introduction.

"Mother, Daniel lives on a different world."

Her mother interrupted, "All men of substance live in their own world."

"No mother, what I meant literary in another world, not on Earth."

For a few moment her mother was confused.

"What do you mean, is he not human?"

"He is human but..," she stopped, "Can't explain, it is a long story, what matters is that he is human, flesh and blood like you and I."

"As long as he is of flesh and blood, I don't care where he comes from, he must be from Australia."

Her father was listening quietly and let the women finish their bickering.

"Tell me young man, do you like it up there?" The father put it lightly.

Daniel was not sure what he meant, "Did he mean the world I live in?"

"Yes sir."

"Daniel, I have read a lot of science fiction novels, and what Fiona is portraying you as an unusual male of her imagination. She has the right to picture you as an outstanding person. I don't blame her judgement of you. To her, you must be out of this world." He said with a wink.

Daniel did not know how to answer that question, but decided to make it clear to them that he actually lives physically in another world, other than Earth. He began with a brief explanation of how events led him to join a team of experts to help some extra-terrestrial beings to solve a problem here on Earth and after doing so the team was given a choice to join them and live on their planet, sandwiched between Jupiter and Saturn.

He also explained how their planet happened to be there.

Fiona's father and mother were lost for words, they just kept staring at Daniel. The father dismissed what Daniel had narrated as a young man's fantasy, but thought of playing along. "What is it called?" He looked squarely at Daniel.

"Urna." Was his prompt reply.

"Do they have women there?"

"Yes, they are just like us in looks, surprisingly they have a lot in common with us, and you might call it a twin Earth."

"Fascinating, and did you chose a wife there?"

The mother looked squarely at the father, "Come on, what a question to ask."

"I can answer that question, no I have no wife, and don't intend to have one."

The mother looked at him, then gazed at Fiona. Before she could say anything, Fiona interrupted.

"Don't think of it mother, we are just friend work together on a special mission."

"Must be an extra-terrestrial affair," the father put in softly with a smile.

"Father, you know with whom I work. All that we do is strictly confidential. Now to change the subject, how are you both doing? Did you hear from Malcolm lately?"

"Your brother is somewhere in Africa, last we heard from him was in Zambia. Working on a dam project. He is doing well. Perhaps he will be here for Christmas."

Informal conversation continued for some time when Fiona looked at her watch and decided to leave.

"Hope to see you again young man before you leave for Una."

"Urna," Daniel corrected him.

In the car Fiona apologised for her parent's point blank behaviour.

"Nothing to worry about, all parents are the same." Daniel said.

"We are going to a friend of mine, haven't seen her in years. She lives close by." She drove and parked her car in front of the gate.

They could hear loud music. Rang the doorbell, no answer. Rang again and waited. "With that commotion inside, no one will hear it."

But then the door opened, "Yes," an instant recognition.

"Fiona, my long lost friend, what do we owe this visit, come right in and who is this gorgeous friend of yours?"

"Daniel, meet my dear friend Jennet," Fiona introduced.

"We are having a little celebration, a friend of ours just got promoted." With a loud voice she announced their entrance, the party continued.

Someone walked up to Daniel. "Your face looks familiar, aren't you Father Daniel. I am Joe."

"Yes I am, Just Daniel now."

"You were reported to have been high jacked by some UFO. I have often visited that church you used to run, there I saw your photograph in a glass box with the mysterious artifacts you found in the church. So glad to meet you, after all the rumours were wrong, you are very much here, tell me what you do for a living."

Daniel was not sure how to answer him. "I have taken a job abroad."

"Still preaching I take it?"

"In a way, it is a long story." They were interrupted by Fiona's appearance, "May I borrow him for a minute," as they walked away she whispered, "That man is a newspaper correspondent and he is the inquisitive type."

"Yes he was asking many questions, you saved me. How about a dance that should keep him away, at least for a while." Daniel suggested.

"I told Jennet briefly what we do, and seeing you with him she suggested I come to your rescue."

"You were on time, thank you." They danced and danced without a stop when suddenly the music stopped and dinner was announced.

The last couple left just after midnight. "It is late to wake up your family, why don't you spend the night here. I have two spare rooms. Go in the morning after breakfast. We can spend some time talking of our younger days."

Daniel retired, Jennet and Fiona composed themselves on a sofas and continued chatting until the early hours of the morning.

Fiona was shown to a bedroom, "Wake me about nine, I need a good sleep,"

Meanwhile, Joe, the newspaper man, sat in his car waiting for Daniel and Fiona to leave. He was curious about Daniel's activity, was not satisfied with what he had told him about working abroad. He was suspicious and wanted to follow them and see where they lived. Hours passed and he patiently waited in his car. Sleep over came him and with the morning traffic he woke up with a jolt. He saw one car parked in front of Jennet's house, "That is the same car since last night, must be Daniel's or the lady's." He said to himself.

He waited tolerantly and to his luck saw the couple walk out of the house with Jennet hugging Fiona good bye. "Now don't disappear, keep in touch and good luck with your project."

Lying low in his seat not to be seen, kept his ears open to hear conversation.

He followed their car. As they stopped near a gate, he parked a little distance away and waited. Someone came and opened the gate wide and the car drove in.

"So that is where they live." Joe muttered.

Daniel and Fiona's car entered and the gatekeeper with a remote activated a sliding panel on the ground that allowed their car to drive through and retracted back.

The newspaper man walked up, there was no nameplate nor the man who had let them in. He looked through the gate and saw an open field with no building or any sign of life anywhere. "Now where did they go?" He murmured.

He walked up and down the road, high trees and bushes obstructed his view.

A hidden camera was monitoring his every move. He was spotted by the Facility security. Out of nowhere a loud growl like a lion's roar sent shivers up his spine, frightened and baffled ran to his car. But he was not to be sent away easily. He sat in his car thinking for a while and later decided to give up. He drove away quickly and swore to come back another day.

Fiona was told of the intruder, "We have had such inquisitive visitors before, nothing to worry about. We know how to handle them." Aishtra comforted her and added "We are all here accept Jim, he should be back by tomorrow latest." Minutes later Jim made an entrance with a jovial gesture, "I am free from all my obligations here, said my good byes for good."

Fiona went out into the garden and sat alone. Her mind was active. "What a life I am getting into, is it real or am I wanting it to be so. All these people here are happy and genuinely care for the welfare of this world, and for them to decide to live in an alien world must be worthwhile. Should I get involved if I am given a chance to join them? My parents are getting on and there is always my bother to look after them."

Jim walked into the garden, "You are all alone, may I join you, I am so happy today and want to get back to my wife, she is all alone out there."

"How is she liking it up there?"

"She is on top of the world out there. Living in Shangri-La if you know what I mean."

That remark penetrated Fiona's head and almost half decided to join the group if given the choice.

CHAPTER 19

In Ayond's garden many feet underground, it was as bright as a sunny day above out in the open. A large round table with well cushioned chairs under a large branch of a tree that covered it. She and her team sat, sipping tea and chatted informally.

Ayond looked at Fiona, "I hope you approve of our hospitality. Are you comfortable?"

Fiona just said, "More than comfortable. I love it here."

"Very good, now let's get down to business. During the past week I have visited many countries and studied the nature of their problems. They are of different types but to sum it up the underline issues are more or less the same. Power hungry and distrusting. Some minorities with different religious beliefs or belonging to different ethnic groups are being prosecuted. The sufferings are unimaginable.

"The super powers are happy to supply weapons to earn money. Knowingly or unknowingly they have given them the muscle to flout it as they please on the poor and weaker nations or ethnic minorities. Great cities of established cultures look like battle fields, millions of people are uprooted from their homes, men women and children are in a pathetic state. Some are on the verge of starvation and inflicted with disease.

"Sitting on a table to discuss a solution may work for some time but knowing the traits of the powerful and the mighty, habits will always come back. We must have a permanent solution, and I do have a plan.

"I want you all to think of what I have said and in a few days want your personal opinions as to what you think should be done, or leave Earth, go back home and let them sort out their own predicament. But not this time, this world is a beautiful place and would not like it to go to waste because of some barbaric incompetent ignorant fools who have no love or sympathy for the rest of mankind and can get away with it.

"Earth was and is our home, now rightfully inherited it after we annihilated the dooms day asteroid. We are the guardians and can put any laws to govern, like a headmaster in a school." Ayond concluded with a worried face.

She sat quietly and studied the faces of each member of the team, then with a soft tone she said, "Now don't look glum, it is not yet the end of the world. Now tell me what you have all been doing while I was away."

They became more at ease and opened up.

She listened attentively of their sojourns out of the Facility.

"Glad you all had a good time, just wanted to check as to how you are faring, we will meet again at my quarters, the day after at eleven in the morning. She turned to Fiona, "How are you getting along, like working with us?"

Fiona had a smile on her face, "O yes, at first didn't think I will fit in, but spending time with these noble gentlemen, learnt how to be happy and useful. Certainly would like to be part of your team."

"You are a pure soul and love to have you with us. Many things you will learn in due course, I will personally teach you some of our ways."

Ayond shook her hand and waved to the rest as they left.

They all got together in David's room. Daniel and Jim chose to go out into the garden, moments later the rest followed.

"Can't imagine we are sitting down here, in a garden in sunshine just like being up there." Fiona remarked as she settled down on a bench next to Jim.

"What do you think of today's meeting," He casually remarked.

"I think it was great, Ayond made a point, her views make sense, and it is not easy to correct the whole world. On whose side she will act, come to think of it, all sides are at fault in different ways. I have no answer."

"I agree with you Fiona, but she wants suggestions from us. I too have no answer." Jim said.

David walked up to them, "What are you talking about. May I join in?"

"We are were talking about what Ayond had said," Jim said and made room for David to sit.

"It is difficult to suggest any thing right now, we'll sleep over it, and perhaps the others may have an answer." David waved to Sam who was pacing up and down on the lawn.

"Sam, I was quite impressed by the treatment Aishtra gave Michael. How about me getting some of that fountain of youth massage."

"David you don't need it, on Urna the climate and water will give you that. In ten years living there you have not aged a bit."

Fiona was listening attentively, "Do you mean no body ages there. Like the mythical Shangri-La."

"Even better, the average age on Urna is about 500 years."

"Ayond looks in her forties, I wonder how old is she by their calendar year?"

"I can't guess, and Aishtra is not from Urna but Earth and she comes from the Jinn race, they too live very long. Aishtra looks in her twenties but she is perhaps much older. Don't tell her that I said that," Sam added in a whisper.

"Fascinating, how lucky you all are. I envy you."

"Fiona, you can have it all, why not come with us."

"Yes and no, I am afraid to feel lonely there."

"We are with you, may find you a husband." Sam said tunefully.

Daniel interrupted, "Don't let them bully you, you better come with me and enjoy a little walk."

They walked to the far end and sat down on a bench. Daniel began, "I owe it all to Sam, had he not got me involved in their project ten years back I would have been still serving the holy communion in that church, still oblivious of the world I have found. Now I feel like a true being, part of an unlimited knowledge and perhaps have been blessed with divine touch."

"You are a sensitive person, easily grasped the gifts you were given. I have not been there but from you I have learned much from your thoughts as if indoctrinated into me. Forgive me for saying this, but subconsciously I have become attached to you, spiritually," Fiona put in gently.

"What are you saying Fiona, I am not a holy apostle. Just a man who now understands what life is about."

Shortly afterwards they dispersed and each went to their rooms.

CHAPTER 20

Sitting in the lush lawn in Ayond's quarters the team sat nervously waiting to hear what Ayond has to say. She looked at each of them as if reading their minds and then with a merry smile, "Blank faces I see before me. It looks like you have nothing to contribute. Why not give it a try, anyone?"

Fiona examined the faces of the team and put in very gently, "I just have one observation to make. After our *heavenly displays,* obviously the people will be recovering from the trauma of the 'supernatural' event, don't you think there has to be a calming effect to guide them to a *new order* to follow."

Ayond promptly replied, "Fiona that is a valid suggestion. I do have a solution, and coming from you strengthens my view, and may improve upon it."

David shook his head affirmatively, "I would like to hear you first Ayond, that might help my brain to contribute some more."

Ayond looked at the rest, discretely all shook their head negatively.

"Let's leave that subject for some other time, for now I will explain step by step the entire line of action to be taken regarding our supernatural displays, and the rolls Aishtra and Fiona will play. Steve and Justin would join us as observers.

Daniel suggested that Bill might enjoy the ride, "After all he is the Prime Minister."

Ayond agreed and would leave it to Steve to invite him.

She moved on to say that the operation is to start two weeks from now, on a Friday through Sunday, when most people have their weekend holidays. But Aishtra's part will begin a week before. She explained step by step her theatrical act starting from the war torn Middle East and move on west, into north Africa. A week later my part will begin, starting from Libya. I will not go into that right now, you will be on board to witness what I have in mind."

A short documentary was shown on life on Urna for the benefit of Fiona.

A week later, Aishtra was escorted by Ayond and Sam to a hanger where they boarded a small craft.

"We will land on the outskirts of a city in Iraq just about dawn, in time for their morning prayers and leave you there. You hop from one city to another, then move on to Syria, Jordan, Egypt and Libya. Next Thursday midday I will meet you with the team, Steve, Justin and perhaps Bill might join us, on the outskirts of the Moroccan city of Rabat, a beam of light to indicate our location.

Aishtra changed her form to an old man, six feet tall holding a walking stick that looked like a roughly shaped branch of a tree. The ship was invisible, she stepped out a few feet from some men heading to a mosque. Seeing the old man appear out of nowhere, they stopped and gazed, then moved cautiously, "Who are you and where have you come from?" One of the men asked loudly with a slight tremble in his voice.

In a commanding masculine voice, the old man replied in Arabic, "I have been sent to warn you all of the punishment that would come soon for the wicked behaviour your people are inflicting upon the weak and helpless, there is time to repent, and judgement day will be soon."

With those words, the old man vanished. The elderly men stood confused, looked to their right and left, fear gripped them, uttering some holy words, hurriedly doubled their pace. At the gate of the mosque the old man waited for them, "Do not forget to tell your people of the warning I have given you." Seeing him again, they hastily wobbled in, some tripped and fell to the ground.

People gathered to help, they told their story, but was dismissed as a hallucination by feeble old men.

Aishtra in her disguise as an old man wanted to have more fun. The mischievous Jinn element within prompted her to play a practical joke. Waited for the prayers to finish, changed to a young beautiful woman, ruffled her hair, swept across the crowd like a missile and stood before the same old men. Kissed each one of them on the cheeks. "Do not forget what I said to you," she whispered with an eerie vocal display and vanished. The bewildered onlookers were horrified, and began to chant religious verses.

The nervous and distraught elderly man narrated their earlier experience that morning and the warning of punishment for their acts of violence.

The news spread, many thought it to be a figment of senile men's imagination, but the few who had witnessed it, took it seriously.

"We are already being punished for being different from the rest as a minority, and in the process of their punishment we too will suffer." One said to his friend who was having tea sitting outside his mud house.

The other replied, "It is an unfair situation, we are a minority, poor and weak, have no place in this world. The rich and powerful and even the corrupt will somehow escape the wrath that is due to come."

A female's voice from inside the house called to come in for breakfast. The men got up, and one invited the other to join him but excused himself and parted.

Meanwhile, Aishtra moved to a large city. The same tall old man appeared. Stood next to the entrance of a bank and kept speaking as if to himself, "What will they do with all this money when the punishment comes? The rich and poor alike will feel the fury that is to come." Someone stopped and looked at the tall figure. "What are you saying my good man."

The old man kept repeating, "The punishment is coming."

"What punishment and by whom?" He asked.

"Your punishment for destroying each other. Wars has become your past time, and you have encouraged the corrupt to wage war on your people and others."

The man walked away, "You are crazy." He shouted.

"Just remember what I said, it will be too late to repent and ask for forgiveness now while you can." The old man said and disappeared.

"Where have you gone, in the name of God who are you?" The man stood still and looked all around and with a hurried pace rushed to a nearby tea shop. "Did you see that, an angel or a mysterious apparition of some kind has warned us of an oncoming punishment for our bad deeds."

Someone commented, "Leave him alone, he must be delirious or seen a mirage."

Aishtra moved to another location, a crowded market place. She repeated her slogans loud enough for the public to hear.

Word spread, people kept talking about a strange man foretelling doomsday, appearing at different places almost at the same time.

Aishtra hopped to Syria and performed the same act. In one location she was pelted with stones.

She hoped to neighbouring Turkey and Eastern Europe and repeated her calls. In Afghanistan and south Asia the old man was treated with respect, and on seeing his disappearing act, the message he conveyed registered firmly in their minds.

Her final round was the North African countries. The old man was ignored and people went about their business, thinking him to be self-proclaimed messiah.

A television announcement said that a mysterious old man has been seen in many countries foretelling doomsday, unless we stop fighting each other. "Many such imposters walk on our streets to cause a commotion. Pay no heed." Was the transmission bulletin.

On her last lag, Aishtra landed in Morocco as the tall old man. An item on the front page of a newspaper said something pleasant about him. "Whoever he is and what he is foretelling should be taken seriously. In this country we respect such people, he may or may not be for real, but all the same there is sense in what he is saying. What people are doing to each other is crazy. Thank God we are not participants in any wars."

Aishtra read the article and decided to go to the appointed place, and wait for Ayond's arrival.

CHAPTER 21

In London, Ayond and her team with Steve and Justin stood outside the mothership, they looked up at the towering structure. They walked in through a small doorway. An elevator took them to the command centre. Ayond sat in front of a host of instruments and a large screen. She swivelled her chair and addressed her entourage that were seated in a semi-circle behind her.

"As we travel, on this screen you will see what is happening outside. You can also choose to sit by a window if you like. While I am sitting on this chair no one is to talk or distract me. Only when I get up from that chair, you may talk to me. This is important."

She whirled her chair and with a wave of a hand she cried loud, "Here we go!"

The ship made a gentle buzzing sound and began to ascend. Moments later the city of London began to fade away. On the screen they could read that they were fifty-five thousand feet high. The sky was dark.

Soon they were over the Mediterranean Sea and descended outside the city of Rabat, in Morocco and beamed its flashing lights to indicate their location. Seeing it, Aishtra glided to meet them.

"How was your sojourn at those places?" Ayond asked.

"One thing for sure, being a Jinn, appearing and disappearing in different location almost spontaneously confused the masses. Only the supernatural can achieve such feats, and that had them guessing. A Moroccan newspaper described it well; an element of the extra-ordinary had imbued," Aishtra observed.

"Well done Aishtra, now you relax while I do my part."

The ship rose and gently drifted eastward. An announcement said, "We will descend to about five hundred feet above the Algerian Sahara where we will stay put for some time."

Some sat beside windows, the other preferred to watch the screen.

The sun shone bright and they could see the desert approaching. The mothership stopped several hundred feet from the ground, below, a lifeless world that stretched endlessly in all directions. Dunes of different shapes and sizes sculptured the topography. A caravan of camels suddenly appeared, sluggishly ambled westwards.

Ayond's voice announced, "We have to wait until the caravan is at a safe distance. They will be able to see what is coming. The disturbed desert will not cause any harm to them."

The wait was long and frustrating.

A loud whirling sound broke the stillness, the sand dunes began to stir and agitate, churning like a giant whirlpool rising upward to form an awesome spiral pillar of sand hundreds of feet high. The ship gently moved eastward with a trail of irate dust particles spreading as far as the eye could see. The murky brown haze on the outside began to obstruct the sun's powerful gaze, the atmosphere became dull and eerie.

The tone of the whirling sound began to change, more like a giant fan turning and scooping tons of more sand upwards, the outside had turned cavernous brown. The ship moved on and the trail of the suspended Sahara followed.

Crossing over Libya, on to Egypt, Israel, Syria, Iraq and Iran, the ghastly scene enveloped the entire landscape.

The ship moved northward on to Turkey, then back southward to Syria, Jordan and Saudi Arabia. Television bulletins from countries effected asked people to remain indoors predicting the freak sand storm would subside in a day or two.

A Saudi television station put it mildly, "Nothing to worry and be alarmed, there have been many such storms in the past, our highly skilled metrological department has predicted that it will pass in a couple days."

"But they are in for a surprise," Ayond put in softly, "Natural winds will take it beyond Iran, now we go back to where we started from, and shall teach those thick skinned a lesson or two, with something more dramatic."

From Algiers, the already disturbed atmosphere was seeded with electrically charged chemical particles that would form a dark viscous brew and fall as droplets with a foul smell like rotten eggs, accompanied by flashes of light and faint sounds of thunder.

Just above the horrifying canopy, the ship gently moved on eastward feeding the suspended dust as far as Iraq.

Soon the chemistry of the concoction began to perform. The shower of black droplets with its rotten odour sent people running madly for shelter. The ship dropped to a level where they could see the scenes below.

Ayond landed the ship in a remote location somewhere in Iraq. "The winds will take it as far as Thailand. "We are in no hurry, spend some time here and listen to television broadcasts. We have sufficient activities on board to keep us busy." She said.

Some broadcasts dismissed it as a unique phenomenon caused by pollution and will pass soon, while some humbly submitted as an act of God, a reprimand for their wrong doings. "That is what I like to hear, but for the non-believers, just you wait I have some more tricks up my sleeve.

A couple of days later, the ship lifted off and moved over to one of the large town in northern Syria. Being invisible no one can see the source of the beam of light focused on to the suspended sullied sand particles, a monstrous hologram showed the distorted unearthly features of Aishtra and Fiona with piercing red eyes and flaming tails stretching across as far as the eye can see.

Despite of the black rain and foul smell, people came out cautiously of their homes with umbrellas, head and face covered, to look at the horrendous images. They gazed in horror and searched around to find the source, as there was none, triggered a sense of reverential fear. Then all of a sudden, the forms dropped to street level and teasingly caressed the onlookers, sent them running in panic. To add more to the spectacle, flashes of blinding light and sounds of thunder resonant from above.

Back safely in their homes, they loudly chanted prayers. The entire neighbourhood reverberated with their surrender to the Almighty.

Satisfied with what she had seen and heard, Ayond moved on to Damascus. The same performance was repeated and the same reaction from the populace. She descended in one her small crafts, being invisible parked not too far from a crowed street. One of the crew who understood Arabic was sent out to hear their reaction. When he returned Ayond was thrilled at what he had to say. "From what I gathered, they seemed terrified, a chastisement for wrong doings, and some shouted judgement day at hand, the old man was right." She thanked him and returned to the mothership.

She decided to replay the hologram as a finale. "It is more appropriate at this moment."

From above the crowed street Fiona stretched across the murky cloud like vapours, flying acrobatically with ruffled hair, skeletal facial expression and piercing red eyes playfully swept down on to the onlookers with a vocal creepy oozing hisses accompanied by flashed of brilliant light and blasts of deafening thunder.

More fearful cries from crowds, they began to disperse and chanted prayers as they ran in all directions.

"I am in the mood for more fun in some other locations," Ayond said. Flew to Iran, Afghanistan, Myanmar Thailand and Malaysia displaying the antics of the hologram.

Next was Africa, starting with Ethiopia, Sudan, Egypt and Libya. There was panic and chaos, some went to the extent of attacking government buildings and institutions blaming them for bringing a curse to the people.

Parked somewhere in the Saharan desert, Ayond waited for more reactions. One television station reported, "A unique black cloud covered the whole of the Middle East, Asia and most of North Africa, accompanied by a tar like rain. Weather experts believed it is caused by pollution and….." It went on to say that there is no need for alarm and that it will pass.

One station mentioned that people are hallucinating, seeing a female figure in the clouds warning of a catastrophe.

"It is perhaps the lightning and the sound of wind that have fueled their imagination," The broadcast went on to say.

A Malaysian station contradicted those broadcasts and went on to say, "It is a bad omen from a divine power to give up wars and respect our governments. Evil people and their ambitious programmes must stop or we all will be punished."

One broadcast from the Middle East mentioned that in many areas people had turned blind and were advised to stay indoors.

Ayond was not satisfied with those broadcasts and felt that more has to be done. Aishtra was next to perform some tricks.

In her capacity as a Jinn she appeared as the tall old man with a stick on one of streets in Damascus. She walked on deserted roads calling for people to come out and listen. From one window someone responded. "What are you shouting about old man?"

"You have witness just a little of what is in store, soon you will all perish. Stop your wars and surrender your weapons to the authorities, otherwise more fire will come from the sky."

More windows opened and some men began to filter out of their houses half blind with hands stretched, surrounded the old man. With a wave of the stick he vanished.

In a state of panic, they shouted, "There is a curse upon us, let us be wise and accept what the old man had warned."

"He is right, let us rally on the streets to stop this crazy war, all concerned must hand over their weapons, fighting is not an answer."

Aishtra moved to several locations in different countries repeating her act. On her return to the ship, they took off for the same spots Aishtra had visited to see the first-hand reactions. On a number of locations warring factions began to regroup and move towards the towns and cities against the people who were confronting them.

Ayond decided to display some fireworks. From the invisible ship came electric like discharges vaporising the aggressors. Witnesses froze to see the fire power coming out of nowhere. They looked up and all around them but saw no source from where the discharges came. They lifted their hands to the sky in prayer.

There were two more such incidents. The news spread and the remaining factions in some countries threw their arm and ran randomly in all directions.

It was what Ayond had wished for. Sitting with the team sipping tea, she put them at ease, "I know what some of you are thinking. Those guys were no good, they had to be eliminated. There is no other way. The people in general are good. But they too needed a bit of shaking up.

A broadcasts said, "Our holy people have taken up the call to bring peace and requested the authorities to stop fighting. Wars are not an answer, all factions must surrender, and it is the public's duty to report wherever the radicals are hiding."

Similar announcements came in from most countries in the regions.

Ayond was happy, "The rain will continue, day by day less will fall. The life span of those clouds is seven days. The effect of temporary blindness will also ware off. The sun will shine again and let's watch their reactions then."

As a final note, it was just before the setting sun, Ayond took the ship few feet above the murky clouds and sent down an enormous electrical discharge that spread right across the entire region in a capillary action, temporarily turning the gloomy dusk into day.

"This should brighten their darkness for some time. They will take it as a sign. You know how people react when under distress."

The ship began to rise, on the screen, the altitude counter showed fifty five thousand feet. They landed near the hanger in London. Within the hour they were back at the Facility. Ayond suggested to have a couple of days rest to unwind.

Steve and Justin decided to stay a short while with the team.

Steve was the first one to speak. "The way Ayond eliminated the opposition was gruesome, we probably would have done the same, but did not expected from the peace loving aliens."

"True," Justin interjected, "The element of justice takes different forms, even with peace loving aliens. You must remember they too evolved from the original stuff the universe is made of. Some have more of it while others far less. We perhaps have more.

"They may have been like us once upon a time, over the years have perfected their way of life," Justin turned to David, "Tell me, what have you observed in their world?"

David was quick to answer, "A peaceful world, no violence of any sort, everybody minds his or her own business. The reason for that is that everyone is contented. Their system of governance is such. When it comes to improper behaviour such as those reptilian aliens who were robbing gold, or the transgressor we just witnessed, justice was swift."

"It looks like we are in safe hands, what they propose to do might be an answer to our troubles. But will it work?" Justin put in.

"Not only that, but should be lasting," Steve commented.

Steve turned to Fiona, 'You looked dashing in the hologram, with your stretched body and ruffled hair and that piercing voice made my hair stand on ends."

Justin was amused and added, "Let's not forget Aishtra's role. What kind of powers you Jinn have that makes you change your form at will. We must sit sometime and tell me more about your species. Can't imagine you live on Earth side by side us humans and we know nothing about you. I think when your mission here is done, we must spend some time learning about you."

Sam interjected loudly, "Not without a fee."

They all laughed. Minutes later Steve and Justin left.

CHAPTER 22

The British Prime Minister sent invitations to the Russian and Chinese leaders with a request to meet. Neither of the invitees knew of the other's invitation. They were told to meet informally to discuss some extraordinary matters related to, *out of the world issues.*

In an open field a large tent was pitched and high security fence to cover the size of four football grounds.

The first to arrive was the Russian president, he was met by the British Prime Minister, Steve and Justin. He was escorted the tent overlooking a large empty ground, and his accompanying security personnel were driven off to a small tent at the far end, completely sealed off not to view the outside.

The Russian walked around, looked at a big round table with eleven chairs, trying to figure out who else might be joining them. It was not long before the other dignitary, the Chinese leader entered. More confusion in his mind. There were few polite exchanges of words, the two leaders swapped discrete glances, observed diplomatic protocol, and reciprocated with a gentle smile. Back in their minds they questioned, 'why in this remote location and the secrecy of the meeting, are the British contemplating a new strategy?'

Outside the tent a few security guards attached to Steve's department, stood vigilant.

Seeing the anxiety on the faces of his guests, the British Prime Minister broke the impasse. "It shan't be long now, our other guests shall be arriving soon."

"What other guests? Perhaps the Americans, the Germans and other western leaders. But there are only eleven chairs?" The Russian was not at ease.

The Chinese paced up and down with a fixed gentle polite smile, he too was not at ease, and kept speculating. "A bit odd for the British to act this way, perhaps planning a new world strategy." His thoughts were interrupted when Steve walked up to them carrying a tray, on which dark glasses neatly laid out and requested them to take one.

Some more confusion on the faces of the leaders.

"I hope this is not a circus tent we are in, some kind of British humour," The Russian was not amused.

Steve politely led them outside, the two leaders stood puzzled facing an empty ground.

Moments later, not far from them, they could see people materialising out of thin air.

"Who or what are those people appearing from nowhere?" The Chinese leader asked hysterically.

"Bill, what drama are you staging for us? Is it some kind of a magic show you are performing for us?" The Russian said with a laugh.

"Please put on your glasses and see for yourselves." Bill requested.

To their amazement and disbelief, both uttered a spontaneous sound of surprize, almost simultaneously exclaimed, "What is that!"

Not far from them the mothership stood in its full majesty, from which human forms are disembarking from it. A waiting vehicle drove them he tent.

"What is it, did you build this and is that the crew of whatever it is?" The Russian looked at Bill, and spoke softly.

"No, we did not build it, in a moment you will meet who did."

The vehicle drove up to them. One by one they stepped out, The Prime Minister walked up to Ayond and led her to the bewildered Russian and Chinese leaders. "This is Ayond, an alien from the planet Urna and *that is* her space ship," pointing at it.

"You must be joking, an alien from another world and looks like us," the Russian said with a bit of a laugh. "You British have a strange sense of humour,"

Ayond's immediate response, "Correction your Excellency, that ship is mine and I am an alien. What did you expect a green creature with claws and red eyes. You will be surprised that there are many life forms better looking than you and us."

The Russian' immediate response, "I am sorry, did not mean to be disrespectful, just an element of surprise. Suddenly coming face to face with an enormous structure and meet an extra-terrestrial being, obviously astonished me. To have a space ship that size and to turn it invisible must be out of this world."

The Chinese shook hands with a wide smile and a gentle bow.

Then the Prime Minister introduced the rest, each one by name, and added that they were from Earth but live in their world. The Chinese leader on shaking hands with Aishtra, commented, "You have beautiful eyes."

Aishtra guessed that he spotted the pupil of her eyes, "Thank you, Sir." She said with a polite smile.

They entered the tent and took their places on the round table. Steve began with a brief introduction about how the planet Urna came to be in the solar system and how the aliens came to Earth fifteen thousand years before and stayed on until about ten years ago when they decided to leave at the peak of the Middle East crises and the fiasco at the United Nations. He also reminded them of the virus that plagued half the world, and their contribution to wipe it out.

"They returned only a short time ago to check on us. Perhaps it is fresh in your minds about the panic caused when observatories worldwide announced the coming of an asteroid that would eliminate all life on this planet. The news was falsified by the Jodrell Bank observatory, to prevent uncontrollable terror and chaos among the masses, though the former announcement was correct. An asteroid was heading towards us, and Madame Ayond and her people destroyed it. Had they not done so, we would not be sitting here today."

The Chinese Leader interrupted, "We saw it too for a while, then it disappeared and we thought we made a mistake in our observation that is why we did not report it in the newspapers. Sorry for the interruption, please continue."

Steve began and narrated that another life form of aliens had come to Earth and were robbing gold and had put up a satellite to control our mind by hypnosis. "They were eradicated by the Lady sitting here, Madame Ayond. Its effect will soon wear out once it is disabled." He concluded by explaining the actions taken in the Middle East a few days ago to put the fear of God into the warring factions. "The aliens thought it best to use supernatural displays. Such theatrics would remind them of the biblical events, like the floods and the punishment of Sodom and Gomorra to make it easier to pave a way to sit on a conference table and listen to what she has to offer.

"Before doing that we thought of inviting your excellences and brief you about how we can bring sanity to our world. You both represent great nations, have a culture going back thousands of years, can add to our efforts in helping this cause. The same will be offered to the western powers." Steve concluded and requested the Russian leader if he had any comments.

The Russian shuffled in his chair and began. He thanked Ayond for saving the world and moved on to say that certain nations act discretely encouraging trouble within countries for their economic and political gains. "We also are no saints, we do have our interests. World politics is dirty, every nation looks for what is best for itself. I do remember reading about the debacle at the United Nations ten years ago, we had our doubts about the authenticity of the alien bit, thought it to be a western conspiracy to control the world, though we were double minded how to react. Almost decided to give our support but decided to abstain as most countries, even some of the western governments just kept silent. That's why your mission failed Madame Ayond.

"I personally, and many in my country are sick of wars in any form, but at the same time no one should be one sided and get bullied by the so called democratic values of conniving leaders to impose their interest on us. I am sorry to look at it that way, but be fair to judge for yourself.

"Nations with accepted political boundaries, freedom to trade and exchange knowledge for the betterment of all mankind would be ideal to live in harmony and peace. Greed in all its forms must be eliminated, only then we can have a workable solution." He concluded and looked at the Chinese Leader.

Ayond stood up and clapped, "Well-spoken your Excellency, I can see the honesty and wisdom in what you have said. It will go well with what I am going to propose in this meeting, but before that I would like to hear what the noble Chinese has to say."

The Chinese Leader was brief. "We are in the process of building our nation economically, whatever political system we use is best for our people. Our country is large and have varied social complexities, it takes time to smooth out the archaic thinking and decadent styles of living, and in due course we will be as good as any other, if not better. We have to follow our methods of governance, we will support any decision so long as it does not interfere with our internal affairs.

"To have a peaceful co-existence is everyone's dream, but perhaps at present it is not possible. You will have to introduce new form of rules all nations must accept with a certain central authority of governance to have peace once for all. Thank you for listening."

Ayond stood up and applauded.

"I have heard the most brilliant words ever spoken by our noble guests and now I may have your permission to say a few words," Ayond began.

"What I have in mind as a solution to start with, summing up to what has been said, you may have said it in a different way, is to introduce a *New World Order*. By this I mean other things remaining the same, a world body will be formed to watch over the activities of each and every nation to behave in a gentlemanly fashion.

"Something like the United States or the Russian Federation. Of course rules suitable to such governance must be acceptable to all parties. It will not be easy but nations who have the sphere of influence on regions can contribute to achieve that goal. It will not be easy, rules has to be made against those not accepting and in the event they do certain conditions has to be fulfilled.

"About religion and freedom of worship, no nation or group shall impose their faith on others. Religion should be a personal thing and respected as such. Whatever you believe in is your choice. No one to impose on others their faith. Those who do not follow the rules, heavy sanctioned will be imposed on them."

"The New World Order will be ruled by nine executive members selected from the world body alphabetically for a period of ten years. In addition, there will be five permanent members who will be the first to accept this order. Any of the five permanent members can vacate their seat/s in favour of another nation or nations provided the remaining members give their unanimous consent. The five permanent members will act as a sentry over the nine members and see to its performance impartially.

Initially there will be one individual selected by us to be the head and final word in all decisions made by the nine elected and five permanent members. Why so, remember we have inherited the guardianship of this world by giving you a new lease to be alive today, without us you would not be here today. Sorry to put it that way, but it is a fact. What we are trying to do is for the good of all mankind."

"I will put the same proposal to the Western powers and then we all meet to form a body to work out the details. For now that is all from me," Ayond concluded.

"What if they refuse to accept," The Chinese leader asked.

"No nation in its right senses will refuse, they will be the losers, you leave it to me," Ayond replied in a firm tone. Then she added, "The New World Order will be the Earth Rule and after a certain period of time membership will be closed. Anyone who refuses to join will be black listed by the member nations and if they decide to join, they will be admitted after ten years during which time certain conditions have to be fulfilled. That would be up to you to decide what conditions should apply.

'Finally I want to remind you once again, because of the present circumstances you do not have a choice, it is not a threat but a polite way of saying we care for you."

Gradually the meeting turned informal and continued for several hours.

Ayond invited the Russian and Chinese guests to be flown to their countries in the mothership. They gladly accepted.

They agreed to be dropped in a park or an open area.

CHAPTER 23

Ayond chose the location of her meeting with some of the western leaders near the Canadian – U.S. Niagara Falls. "I love both those countries, and especially Canada reminds me of home. The people are friendly and full of smiles. Forgive me, but I am being frank. And I can add, the whole of this continent fascinates me, its topography and the climate which I am sure has something to do with their development." She was talking to Steve privately while planning their next move.

Confidentially invitations were sent to the United States, Canada, Mexico, Brazil, Japan, Australia, New Zealand, South Africa and Germany. No one was told of the agenda of the meeting and who were invited. It was just a request by the British Prime Minister to spend some time discussing topics related to *the understanding of a better world*.

Not far from the Niagara Falls, in an open ground a tent was pitched in which a large round table with chairs. On one side, a table with a host of refreshments. At the far end of the ground, especially tailored tent with no windows and a secured door that could not be opened from the inside, was to host any security personal accompanying a leader.

On the scheduled date, one after another the VIP aircrafts landed at Toronto airport and were met by the British and Canadian Prime Ministers. Only the heads of states were ferried by helicopters to the meeting place, accompanies only by one of their security staff, who on arrival was taken to the especially tailored tent. Only security personal belonging to Steve's department kept a strict vigilance.

As the guessed filtered in, they were surprised to see the other leaders as they were not told beforehand who were invited. However, they socialised and wondered what the meeting was about. Some termed it as a practical joke by the Canadians. "I heard that remark, no it is not a joke, we did what the British Prime Minister requested us to prepare. I, myself have no idea what for," The Canadian Prime Minister clarified his position. Soft music played in the background.

The music stopped and Steve made an announcement. "Ladies and gentlemen, may I have your attention please, I would request you to come outside. Our very special guest for whom we are assembled here has arrived."

"What special guest is he talking about?" someone asked loudly.

"I will answer that." The British Prime Minister said. "Just follow me and soon you will see for yourself."

Outside they lined up, the British Prime Minister stood further ahead with his back towards them. All the attendees looked confused, exchanged quizzical glances. He then turned around wearing dark glasses. It added more to the puzzle. Steve stepped forward with a tray in which there were similar dark glasses and approached them, "Please take one and don't wear it until I say so." He said to each person as they picked one. They were more confused and some exchanged wide smiles with dramatic facial expressions.

"Now please put them on,' Steve requested. Before them not a hundred feet away, stood a shining brassy wall. Soon its appearance dawned on them that they were staring at a very large, what looked like a spaceship.

Baffled and astonished, they were in a state of shock and disbelief. A door opened and a ramp extended outwards, out came Ayond with her team. Someone said loudly, "What in the world is that and who are those people coming out of it?"

Steve announced proudly, "Ladies and gentlemen that is a spaceship from another world and soon you will meet its occupants."

"But they look human to me, they don't look like aliens." Someone said.

"Excuse me sir, have you met an alien before?" Steve politely interjected.

"No, but those people look very much human."

"Well, some of them are, please be patient, soon you will meet them and clarify your curiosity." Steve said, accompanied by the British Prime Minister walked toward the vehicle bringing the visitors.

Ayond was the first to step out. Both greeted her, out of the vehicle the rest of her team filed behind her. The British Prime Minister, with a loud voice, "Your excellences, I have the greatest pleasure to welcome Madame Ayond, from the planet Urna, and with her a team from Earth who chose to live with them."

Suspiciously they shook hands with her and allowed a forced polite smile. They were puzzled and half minded.

Ayond read their minds, "I look too human to be an alien from their point of view," she thought.

"Excuse me Madame, is that thing," pointing at the spaceship, "Is that your craft in which you travelled? The Brazilian President asked enquiringly.

"Yes sir," Ayond replied and moved on. "Obviously, how else can I be here?" She said to herself.

The massive structure that stood a few feet away from them, sent a message that they were dealing with an alien visitor far superior to their liking. They humbly but suspiciously followed and took their seats in the tent.

The British Prime Minister introduced each head of state and conversely Ayond her team.

Steve began, "In the brochure in front of you, you have everything you want to know about our alien friend. You can read it at leisure when you get back home. She is not new to our planet as you will soon find out." Steve was interrupted by the president of the United States, addressed the British Prime Minister, "Bill, where have you been hiding these precious people and you know them by their names. Why we were not told beforehand. Such a historic event should have been shared."

His reply was prompt, "Mr. President, Madame Ayond and her predecessors are not new to our world, and they have been here much before our recorded history and have as much claim to our planet as much as we have. In the course of this meeting you will learn why. Now to answer your question, if you remember Mr. President, ten years ago when we came openly with an alien friend at the United Nations, you and the rest of the big powers gave a cold shoulder and did not move a finger to support the cause. Their objectives were noble, to help iron out our confused social infrastructure, and the dangers that lay ahead at that time which was in its infancy, had it been corrected then we would not have suffered the ordeal we have had and still persisting to the present day. However, seeing our non-acceptance then to what they wanted to do for us, they decided to leave and return to their world, leaving us alone to face our predicament." Bill put in politely."

Ayond listened attentively and appreciated what was said. It was the catalyst for her address.

The U.S. president continued, "That was a different time and to be honest with you, I had read the file, our delegation was skeptic about the reality of the alien bit and that deliberation at the United Nations. It sounded too far-fetched to be true. We appreciated the good intention of that meeting, but to come face to face suddenly with an alien we knew nothing about made us suspicious."

"Well, let bygones be bygone. We are here today and before we start, with Madame Ayond's permission, I would request Steve, who is in charge of this mission, to give you a brief summary about our noble visitor and why she has returned. With this background, it will help you to understand the purpose of our meeting." The British Prime Minister said and asked Steve to continue.

"You will find it all in the brochure, but for the sake of this meeting a brief introduction is needed." Steve began from the time planet Urna lost its orbit around its binary system, their arrival on Earth, and why they decided to leave after staying fifteen thousand years on Earth.

He concluded by the recent event about the approaching asteroid and its demise. "Had it not been for them, we all would not be sitting here." Then he added a punch line. "Having saved us from eminent extinction, they have given us a new lease of life."

"Bill, you knew it all along and never considered sharing it with the world," The Brazilian president interjected looking at the British Prime Minister.

"We were under a secret oath not to divulge, however, we are now here and would like you to listen to what Madame Ayond has to say," Bill said and sat down.

Ayond began with a brief introduction of her Earth team and the circumstances that led them to be with her. "But there is one special person in my team, also from your world but not human. Aishtra please stand up."

There was a scuffle of chairs as they all stares at her.

"What kind of joke is this, she looks human like any all of us here.' Someone remarked.

"In appearance, yes. But let her demonstrate one of her capabilities. You will then understand what I am going to tell you."

Ayond asked Aishtra to look like the American president. Which she gladly obliged.

There was a unanimous expression of disbelief. To add more to the bewildered audience, she change to a person everyone remembers, Marilyn Monroe.

Involuntarily they all got up and applauded.

"What kind of magic is this?" The Brazilian president blared out.

"No magic is involved your Excellency, as I am an alien from the planet Urna, she is too of a different species but from your world. She is what you would what call, a Jinn. They are very well known to the people of the Middle and the Far East, in the West they are referred to as demons. They are a gentle race with extra-ordinary powers. They are like humans, have a naughty and aggressive tendencies. You may sit down Aishtra." Ayond said and added, "I can see some of you are fascinated but with a shadow of doubt. Some details of their origin is in the brochures in front of you."

Someone put up his hand, "Sorry to change the subject, why the Russians and Chinese are not invited?"

"That question I cannot answer right now, but soon you will find out. Now let me get down to why we are meeting here today. Ladies and gentlemen let me come to the point," Ayond said with a business like tone, "Your planet had a narrow escape, had it not been for us you would have been a pile of ash. Sorry to put it that way, but facts are facts and must be faced. Check with your observatories. We have been here for a long time, since before your recorded history. We have an equal right to this world as you do. We also know your temperaments, your varied cultures and beliefs, never did we interfere with those and let you solve your problems on your own.

"That *was* in the past. But now it is different. The time has come to correct your past, to a better way. Why and how? Read the brochure given to you, it is explained in details. By virtue of having saved you from an imminent annihilation by an asteroid, we gave you a chance to continue living. That act has made us your saviours and the guardians of your planet, gave us the right to show you how to live in a peaceful manner, whether you like it or not. It is not a threat but to put it nicely, will show you the way.

"We love this world, most of you have not realized its beauty. It is not unique in the Milky Way Galaxy or perhaps in the universe, at least it is so in your solar system and some other systems. Lucky for our planet to became a resident here, so you are not the only life form. Besides, unknown to you there are some others you don't know about. In time, when you qualify as a good neighbour you will meet them, though of course not as attractive.

"Let me tell you briefly how we were added to your solar system, our world is much older than yours, we had a head start of hundreds of thousands of years ……" She narrated the entire story from the time they landed here and their return to their world. "I have come back to tell you how fortunate you all are to be alive after we destroyed that asteroid.

"From a philosophical point of view you no longer exist in this world, but you are still alive because of us. I want you to forget the past ever existed as far as you are concerned. Turn a new page and start all over, with our guidance. You have no choice, we can take over the whole planet and rule it, turn you into some kind of freaks, but we come with a noble cause, to care and provide.

"I therefore, propose to implement a New World Order to govern the entire planet. You will have the right to govern your country without our interfering with your beliefs or your ways, with some conditions which we will implement. Those who do not accept to come into the fold shall be isolated by all nations, no trading, economic or technological assistance and even visitations. Only when they feel the pinch and decide to join, they would qualify, after ten years of good behaviour. That will apply to all nations, big or small. The natural wealth earnings would be spent on the welfare of the state, not go in the pocket of those who rule."

She explained the new world order administrative procedure. "The old ways must go and brace yourselves to accept the new. Those who falter will face the consequences. Trust me, soon you will be happier than you ever have been; I am referring to days before you would have tuned to ashes."

Then she went on to explain the New World Order the way she had to the Russians and Chinese.

"It will not be easy at first, you have different political thoughts, cultures and religions, and each wants to impose its own on others. Unless that decadent and archaic system is abolished there is no way out. Religions are deep rooted and not to be disturbed but will implement a strict ruling that no one religion is to be imposed on others or condemn it. Defaulters will be punishable to the entire community they belong to.

"We will set a time limit to accept members. I will address your United Nations with all the world leaders attending. I need your full support. The Russian and Chinese will join you. I have given you the concept now, it is up to you to study my proposal wisely."

There were many questions, Ayond just answered, "We are not here to debate the issue, just get to work on what I have proposed. You have no choice, remember we are the custodians."

Hours later the conversation turned informal and finally ended with a happy note.
"If your planet is as good as your Earth friend say it is, I must go and see it for myself," The Mexican President said with a loud voice.

"When we think you are ready you will be most welcome," Ayond replied him politely.

As the final note, Ayond took them for a tour of the spaceship. Seeing its size and what it can do, sent a message, a power to reckon with. The Japanese guest asked if they would share their knowledge with humans.

"Why not, but before that you must be ready to accept the good life and the gift you are given in this Garden of Eden, called Earth."

CHAPTER 24

The Western leaders left with a nonchalant attitude, said their goodbyes to their host and the alien visitor with a cold handshake. "Give it a month or two, we are in no hurry, let them digest what I have said, my reading is that all those who attended are men and women of substance. In the long run they will benefit by cutting off those strings of nations on whom billions if not trillions of dollars are spent on aids and military supports and conversely those nations will also gain confidence in self-support and do away with unnecessary spending on military adventures." Ayond soothed the British Prime Minister who looked disheartened.

Two weeks later, the British Prime Minister sat with Steve and Justin to exchange views of how the rest of the world would react.

"I am worried if it does not go well with most countries. They may ridicule the whole exercise and brand it as conspiracy for world domination.

Steve calmly started, "Bill, you are handling a unique situation no other Prime Minister had. World wars in the past were conducted wisely and we came out to be the winners. The situation as it stands today is more complex, we are talking of creating a United States of the world. A new way of life, it will surely have its teething problems. The world has to understand and accept that, had it not been for the aliens we would have gone back to living in caves or eradicated completely. Let it sink in their heads. Only then we can move forward. The change has to come and will come, Ayond will fight for it tooth and nail to achieve it, remember she carries the stick, god forbid, what if comes to using it."

"I agree with Steve, a New World Order has to come, one way or another, it will be wise for the super powers to support and help others to participate. No way out." Justin added.

"True, she also indicated on putting as a head of the New Order, a person of her choice. If she is thinking of putting one of the Super Powers, she is mistaken." Bill said.

"Excuse me Bill, she is thinking of a person who has immense powers, a superman so to speak, they call him the Guardian. He is an artificial intelligence being, No one will dare to oppose him," Steve revealed.

Bill thought for a moment, "That will be the day when an android would rule over us, what a shame; but if he can deliver the goods, why not."

"Ayond's intentions are good, initially the Guardian will smooth all the edges which no one on earth can, and perhaps after a while, an electoral procedure will choose a person from our world. It may take many years but that will surely happen," Steve explained.

"Looks reasonable, I do trust Ayond's intentions, she values our planet, after all she was born here, her Supreme High and Guardian lived here from the time before we humans developed, thousands of years ago," Bill said thoughtfully.

There was a knock on the door and a secretary entered, handed Justin a newspaper with a red circle around a news item.

Justin read it out, "It says, 'World leaders Meet with ETs. A massive spaceship landed near the Niagara Falls in Canada, where they were met by some world leaders," Bill interrupted, "Let me have the papers, I want to read it myself.

He read loud for Justin and Steve to hear, "I like this bit where it says, 'a clandestine meeting with extraterrestrials, it is speculated that a deal was made with the ETs to rule the world. When contacted, some of the world leaders who attended denied the allegation as false and cheap journalism.' Bill threw the paper on the desk, "Now, how did that happen, No one knew what the meeting was about," he paused to think, "Most likely it is one of the security men, there were only ten of them, one with each of the guests, one with me and two Canadians. I am now worried as to how Ayond will react." Bill was not pleased.

Steve was given the responsibility to inform Ayond and to deal with the situation. When contacted, she told him that the news had already reached her and requested him to bring the ten security men who had accompanied their world leaders. "I trust your men Steve, bring me only those ten to Justin's office for an interrogation."

"No reason is to be given to them why they are being called. When they arrive, bring in two undercover men from Scotland Yard as witnesses. You and Justin must be there."

Within a week they arrived and were brought to Justin's Office. They were taken to a room and handed over to two of Ayond's security men. They were asked to strip naked and were made to wear a skin tight outfit. Though confused about the drill they were going through, they obediently complied. A mask with a skull cap was tightly fitted, only the eyes showing through a glass lens.

One of them asked, "What is this all about, a bit uncomfortable."

"Nothing to worry about, it is only for a short time." One of Ayond's security men said.

When all were ready, they were lined up, one of the security men pressed a gadget against each producing a flow of electrical discharge around the entire suit.

"Nothing to worry about, it is harmless and for your safety." They were told.

Being well trained security men, used to drills of all kinds, though this one was different.

A number from one to ten was attached on each person. They were handed to the security men from Scotland Yard and escorted them to the room where Ayond, Steve and Justin waited. They lined up facing them. The Scotland Yard men stood near the entrance.

Ayond began, "Gentlemen, I am sorry for the inconvenience of wearing this outfit, it is a bit of an experiment to verify your integrity, if you answer truthfully, there is nothing to worry about. Do not lie or hesitate. If you do, you will feel discomfort. Be honest.

"When I call your number, I am going to ask you simple questions, you will answer, yes or no, nothing else. Do you all understand what I have said? You will individually answer when I call your number. Raise your right hands if you have understood my instructions," Ayond said firmly.

They all did.

"Number one, were you on security duty at the meeting with your president at the Niagara Falls on the Canadian side?" She asked.

Promptly he answered, "Yes."

She waited a minute, then asked the next person the same question, then the next and so on. All answered in the affirmative.

"My next question, number one. Did you see something unusual like a plane or a spaceship at the meeting place?" His answer was, "No."

All but one answered in the negative.

"What about you number six, you seem to hesitate? Yes or no?"

"Think again, I will come back to you later."

"My next question, number one, did you tell anyone or any group about your mission on that day?'

"No."

She asked all except number six, their answer was, "no."

Number six, you seemed to hesitate to answer a previous question, let me assume that you had seen something, did you disclose it to anyone?

Again there was a slight hesitation, there was a pause and he began to feel some discomfort, touched his head with both hands as if to remove the head mask and in pain said something, "When we were leaving, my president gave me those glasses to hold, I was tempted to wear them and saw the big ship." He stopped, "The mask is hurting me." He said painfully.

"Did you tell anyone about what you saw?"

"Noooo, but they...." He did not complete the sentence and to the horror of those in the room, within an instant his mask began to light up, fumes began to envelope his outfit. Seconds later his body crumbled into a puddle within the suit.

She continued with her questioning, the rest passed without an incident and were allowed to leave.

Steve spoke softly, "Very cruel way to go, but will have an effect on the others to keep their mouths shut in the future."

CHAPTER 25

With a request from the British Prime Minister and other permanent members of the United Nations, the Secretary General sent invitations to all heads of state to attend an emergency meeting of prime importance. The response was encouraging. Only a few nations would be represented by their ambassadors. No details of the meeting were mentioned.

A day before the meeting Bill, Ayond and her team, Steve, and Justin took off for New York.

Tight security surrounded the United Nations building, only cars and occupants who had special electronic passes were permitted within five hundred feet.

Inside, especially the assembly hall was inspected inch by inch physically and by electronic devises. Participants entered after being heavily scrutinised and escorted to their seats.

In the back ground soft music by Respighi, Pachelbel and Albinoni played while members gathered and sat in silence.

"With that music they have said what they have to say'," One of the members remarked to a colleague next to him.

The music soon faded and in a single file from a door near the rostrum, the Russian and Chinese presidents walked in, the members stunned by their appearance, stood up and applauded. Behind them followed the western leaders who had attended the meeting with Ayond. The confused assembly exchanged glances, but continued to clap, turning the hall into a fury of bursts of tuneful ovation. The leaders sat below the podium facing the delegates. Soon the hall came to a pin drop silence.

Almost immediately the Secretary General entered with Ayond and once again the applauses flayed. It took a while to bring the hall to order. He began. "Your royal highnesses, excellences, ladies and gentlemen, it is a historic day for us here and for the people of Earth. I have the great privilege to welcome our noble guest from another world, from the planet Urna, Madame Ayond. Though an alien and yet not so, it is a paradox.

"Let me refresh your memory, some of you may remember ten years ago an alien who had addressed the United Nations with good intentions to advise us how to change the scheme of things for the better and bring harmony and peace to our beautiful world. In response, the majority of the members jeered and some walked out of the hall. It was a bad day. But today history is repeating itself, to something most unexpected and perhaps will set right the rough edges of our wellbeing. After the conclusion of this gathering a pamphlet will be given to you with all the details that will be said here in this meeting. Study it well and treasure it, may illuminate the pathway of what is to come.

"Now I have the pleasure to request our illustrious visitor, Madame Ayond to take the floor."

Ayond thanked the Secretary General and faced the hall, looked at her audience for a few moments, waited until they were in complete receptiveness.

"I am delighted to address this elite gathering, each one of you represents millions of human beings who depend on your guidance to give them a happy home. It is not an easy task, using an old adage, 'uneasy is the head that wears the crown', hope I am quoting it right.

"The Secretary General did not mention that the alien who addressed this body of world representatives ten years ago was me. It is a long story, you will find it in the pamphlet that will be given to you. But no harm in briefing you a little.

"We came to your world by chance, our rough planet drifted in space for many years, and when we spotted Earth, decided to land with as many people as we could. That was fifteen thousand years ago." Ayond went on to explain the contribution they had made to assist the development of mankind and discretely withdrew from the scene some years later to live exclusively without interfering in human affairs.

She also reminded them that they were here when humans were in their early stages of social development, and they had an equal right to live side by side. They decided to leave when their welcome came to an abrupt end at the fiasco at the United Nations and the brewing war.

"Luckily our planet had found a home in your solar system, was drawn by your sun and was put in between Jupiter and Saturn and we went back to it. That was in the past.

Today I am here in a different capacity. Please listen carefully to what I have to say, evaluate each point.

"Some months ago, your planet was threatened by an imminent catastrophe, a giant asteroid was heading your way, on impact the extinction of all life, turning the entire planet into a flaming ball of fire. You would not be here today, but a pile of ash. When we spotted it, special arrangements were made by us and eliminated it. By doing so, in brief, gave you a new lease on life to continue living."

She was interrupted by a standing ovation that seemed unending. She waited patiently in appreciation until it died down.

"Thank you, we did it to save the place we once called home, and by virtue of that, sorry to put it that way, we have inherited the custodianship of this planet. Now I will speak in the past tense, you were plagued with social disorders in many forms which led to wars, sickness and poverty. The past has gone where you would have been in a pile of cinder. Coming to the present tense, that old slate is wiped out completely, we will now begin with a new, like an infant coming to the world oblivious of everything around him, embarking on a journey of hope and prosperity. I want you all to place yourselves as that new born child. Wouldn't that be a happy beginning?"

Ayond paused for her listeners to digest what she had said. There were murmurs and shuffling among the delegates.

"We are here to help you," her voice was loud, "to achieve that goal, will need sacrifices and to do away with old archaic and ignorant thinking. It would be hard at first, old habits die hard, but in this case, as an infant, you do not have that memory of the past. Consider what I have said seriously, because what I propose, is not negotiable. To put your minds at ease, to receive what I am going to say, I suggest an hour's break."

The hall came to life as the delegates walked out to the refreshment room. Ayond and the dignitaries sitting below the rostrum went to private chamber, joined by her team, Steve and Justin. She realised that some of the leaders had worried expressions and were not communicative. She ignored them.

An hour later, the assembly hall recommenced.

After a few pleasant remarks, Ayond began, "I will come to the point, we have decided to implement a type of a universal governance controlled by a body of selected men and women to rule over a new world order. Which means that every country becomes an integral part of a united states of the world. Within your geographical borders you will rule supreme, but under the watchful eyes of the world order. A constitution will spell out the rules.

"Any country or a nation who chooses not to join, will be black listed, no trading, visitations or ambassadorial representation. Should they change their mind, certain rules shall apply." She went on to explain in detail what she had elucidated to the Russian, Chinese and western leaders in their earlier meetings.

"It will be hard in the beginning but if you genuinely make an effort, you will succeed. But if you try to deviate in any way, we will come hard on you. Remember we are your guardians and you would not like it if we get angry.

"You spend trillions of dollars in possessing dangerous weaponry, to kill your fellow human being. Like a child playing with matches, you will realise its potential when you burns yourself. Had you spent those dollars on technology and research, you may have had the capability to destroy that asteroid and any other future threats that may be lurking in the future.

"I will not touch on the subject of faiths or religions. You may do as you please as long as it is confined within your borders. Leave others alone to worship as they please. On interference in other's beliefs, we would come down with a heavy hand. Same goes for imposing forcibly your beliefs on others within your boundaries.

"I have conveyed to you our plan to institute the new world order. When we are ready with the constitution and its bylaws, we will appoint one of our choosing to be its head. He will have unlimited powers and you would not like him to use it, because if he does, god forbid, using your expression, it will be the guilty party's total annihilation. Now I am open to questions." Ayond said and waited.

Someone asked if the aliens had a divine entity.

"Not the way you have. It is more philosophical. What does a divine entity ask of you? To be good and in return you worship him for that advice. Worship is a way to say thank you for the good he bestows. On our planet Urna, which means *happy people*, we have an entity we call the Supreme High. He is all knowing and helps us in bad times and protects us from evil. We do not worship him but hold him in high esteem and he knows that. Because of him we became good, don't have wars or usurp what is not ours. Reason, not emotion is our yard stick. We do not have theatrical acts or attires to impress him, he knows what is in our hearts and minds." She concluded to the stunned audience.

"Any other question?" She asked.

"Prior to the Supreme High, did you have a faith or a religion of some sort?"

Ayond promptly replied, "In a way we had an archaic belief developed out of superstition and ignorance. It began when people started to carry good will charms in the form of pieces of wood, animal bones or a little figurines. Gradually it grew into a cult. Over the years more emerged with different variations. It became like a religion, competition between them grew to the extent that it became political, and opened doors to conflicts. It was hard to control, but with an iron fist of the authorities it died down."

"Any one?" She asked.

"This Supreme High of yours, does he live with you on your planet. What is he, a deity or a holy person?"

"Neither. To be honest, he is a very sophisticated machine, in your world you would call it a super computer. But, he is not just a computer, has the ability to control the weather, the planet's magnetic field, can cause unimaginable fire power at his will, can read minds, what we are thinking, and his abilities are limitless."

"Did you make him?" Someone asked.

"No we did not. It was very long time ago, much before we came to Earth when our planet was stable in a binary system. It was by chance that a highly sophisticated android landed on our world and told us of a super machine that was made by people, like you with flesh and blood. That world became sterile due natural causes. Robots, and androids were made to compensate for the declining population. The android took us to that world and we retrieved that super machine which we renamed, the Supreme High, because of its capabilities. Subsequently, we began treating it as an entity, not as an 'it' but as a 'him'. He has been with us ever since, does not age or show any signs of malfunctions. The android was subsequently given a tile by us, we called him the Guardian and he is in charge of the Supreme High's maintenance. The Guardian too has untold powers, can turn itself into light waves and travel at high speed. He can incinerate a city with a beam of light.

"The Supreme High and the Guardian taught us how to build spaceships far superior than our own with weapons that can shatter your moon. That was how we destroyed the asteroid that threatened your planet." Ayond concluded and was about to end with a closing speech, she was interrupted.

"I have to say a few words, if you allow me? May I have your permission?" A voice rang high.

"Yes please, what do have to say?" Ayond politely replied.

"I am the ruler of a very old kingdom in south East Asia, we go back a thousand years of uninterrupted culture and religious belief. Having heard what has been said, enlightened my way of thinking. Perhaps we are in the same position as your people were prior to your all-knowing Supreme High. I, for one, is most willing to go along with your suggestions and shall adhere to the reforms the new world order would bring. As you rightfully said, our past is no more, we would have incinerated with the imminent asteroid.

It is time to face the truth and turn a new page. I will do all I can to influence friendly nations in my area to comply."

Ayond clapped, "Your Royal Highness," She addressed the Asian King, "I complement you on your brave gesture and pleased to confer upon you as the first permanent member to the new world order."

Seeing the sudden unpredicted dramatic development, that some others may jump in to claim their allegiance and not to be missed out, the Russian and Chinese proclaimed their support, quickly followed by the United States and the United Kingdom.

Ayond was more than pleased and promptly proclaimed, "I am proud to announce the wise decision of these nations, we now have the permanent members. As for the executive nine members who will administer the new world order, I am going to make an exception. As a start to set up the administration, I select the eight remaining members who participated in the initial formal discussion earlier, plus one member country from the United Nations starting with the letter A. Future nine members would be selected from that alphabetical order, thus giving each and every member a chance to operate this new world body of governance.

"All others must register their acceptance to the new world order within two weeks, failing that, sanctions would be imposed. Should they then decide to join, they would be admitted after a period of ten years. Trouble makers would forfeit their status to rule and will be put away on a prison island in solitary confinement for the rest of their lives. Their country would be taken over and run by the new order.

"Finally I would like to add," Ayond moved close to the Secretary General and extended her hand, "Let me congratulate you, for being selected by me as the Secretary General of the New World Order."

A few half-hearted claps sounded from different parts of the hall.

"We conclude our meeting for today and shall meet in two weeks. The Secretary General shall issue the invitations. Think wisely, don't waste this opportunity, because if you do, you will regret it." Ayond voice was firm.

For a few long seconds the hall was in pin drop silence then there was the sound of a single clap, followed by a few, half-heartedly, some more joined, reluctantly.

The Secretary General looked at Ayond and softly remarked, "I have a feeling your message was understood, and perhaps you be returning home sooner than expected."

"I am not so sure, but at least there are a few who genuinely accepted my proposals. I foresee the road ahead of us will not be as smooth as it appears, there are many bumps that will need to be levelled."

CHAPTER 26

Back in London Ayond called a meeting with her team. "You all have witnessed what happened at the United Nations. Any comments?"

Jim cautiously began in a soft spoken way, "Difficult to judge, I am sure there are those who just clapped to keep up with the rest. There will be some hard nuts to crack who will not approve or even consider changing their ways."

"And you David?"

"I agree with Jim, but the super powers can do a lot in the areas of their sphere of influence. Accept or be left out."

Fiona was listening while doodling with a pencil, lifted her head and said, "Ayond's warning was strong enough, if they have registered what she meant. Without joining the club they would be singled out and suffer the consequences. Some may consider joining, just to be in the club, with some devious, conniving agenda and continue their multifarious activities to destabilize the fraternity. If and when they are exposed, their punishment should be exemplary, banished for life and their state taken over and run by the new order, just as Ayond had put it."

"A good observation Fiona, no doubts there will be teething problems at first, and we will have to deal with each case on its merits. The stubborn ones must be dealt with severely. In a few years all will get used to the change and hopefully the new order will survive," Ayond concluded.

The rest were of the same opinion as Fiona. Sam added, "Being a simple building contractor while living here, was proud to see military parades and the display of our weapons that could kill millions. Other nations, big or small, are equally proud to have such displays of instruments of destruction and all are competing with one another. Now I think differently, what is that fuss about? To kill, just because they don't see eye to eye. Trillions of dollars are spent on how to kill and destroy, and the makers of those killing machines are more than happy to oblige, they earn the dollar. What a barbaric way to exist. Ayond has to be tactful with a bit of persuasion to take full control of all the military installations worldwide and be operated only by the new order. It will be used only to police the country in which they are located. Mankind will no longer have the capability to inflict pain and suffering on others."

"I must say Sam, you have become a true believer of our cause, and I have always trusted your judgements." Ayond said appreciably.

"Sometimes I think, is it really worth the effort, why don't we let them reach the point when they blow themselves up, only then they will sit back and reflect that they were wrong." David put in softly.

"There would be no one to sit and reflect, perhaps if some are lucky to survive, they would be thinking how to make a bow and arrow to keep away the others." Jim said cynically.

That night Ayond sat with Argos. Through him a full report was communicated to the Supreme High on Urna.

The next day, Argos informed her of the response from the Supreme High. He asked her to stay on Earth until the completion of the new world order, and to deal with any opposition in a pleasant way depending on regional culture and beliefs. Only should they become hostile, to handle the situation as deem fit.

Ayond contacted all her operative informers worldwide to report any positive or negative reactions about her deliberations at the United Nations. Some reports were satisfactory and some were disturbing.

Mobsters attacked government buildings whose leaders were in favour of the change, they even went to the extent of targeting individuals. Main trouble spots were in South America, Central, South and South East Asia, and the Middle East.

The situation was delicate, but had to be dealt with. A squad of well-trained alien force was despatched in one of the invisible small crafts.

The informers pin pointed the location of the trouble makers and were eradicated. The punishment was swift and severe, it came in its invisible form, and peace to some extent was restored. A lesson was learnt.

Peace loving organizations paraded in praise of the invisible protector. Opposition squads marched against them and blamed the aliens for their high handed merciless actions, but quickly dispersed for fear of reprisal. The informers noted their leaders and reported them. Soon they too received the punisher's wrath. A shaky calm was restored. The *punisher,* wherever there were signs of trouble, acted swiftly.

Ayond felt somewhat relieved, but that was short lived. She received a phone call from an informer operative in Italy.

He conveyed that a secret meeting is scheduled to be held in an obscure little village near Rome, to be attended by the Pope, a senior representatives of the Muslim faith and a Jewish Rabbi. The informer suggested that he would visit the village dressed as a priest representing a church in the neighbourhood. If he is lucky, would try to attend that meeting.

To Ayond it sounded odd for the three religious leaders to meet in a clandestine manner and wondered how the informer would get near them, not to mention getting into that meeting. She scoffed at the idea and gave him her approval and said jokingly, "Be careful, if your cover is exposed they may burn you at the stake or sacrifice you at the altar."

The informer arrived at the village, dressed as priest, came to the premises where the meeting is being held. He was stopped by some plain cloth security men and some priests.

"What can we do for you brother, this is private property." One of the elderly priests asked.

"I look after a church not far from here, word got around about His Holiness's visit to this place, I have to convey personally a very special message, and he would be pleased to hear it. May I be allowed to meet him briefly?"

"What kind of message, and from whom? You may convey it to me and I will deliver it." The priest said.

"No, can't do that. The one who gave me that message explicitly instructed, it should be conveyed in person. It is a matter of survival of our faith."

"Sorry we cannot do that, you can go to Rome after a couple of days and meet me there, I will do my best to arrange a meeting."

"It is up to you, my message cannot wait, but if you insist, I will leave and not to pass on what I have to convey. You may have to bear the consequences." He turned around and began to leave.

The other priests came up and asked, "What does that vagabond wants?"

"Please do not refer to him as a vagabond, he is a priest from some church, he said he has an important message for his Holiness and only he can deliver it."

"He must be one of those crafty ones who look for donations." The other priests said.

"He did not look crafty to me, from his attire, though shabby, he sounded serious about his message." The elder priest replied, and felt a bit of a guilt for turning him away.

To add to that feeling, the other priest said casually, more in humour, "Perhaps he is an angle in human disguise. Whatever he is, we should report it to His Holiness. You know how touchy he is when it comes to poor priests. At least convey the incident to him."

"You may be right, I will go in and tell him, meanwhile run up and bring him back, just in case."

The younger priest dashed and shouted to stop.

The elder priest conveyed the message and His Holiness instructed to bring the mysterious priest to him.

In a dimly lit chapel the Pope sat with the other two representatives of Islam and Judaism at a small table with the three holy books on it.

The mysterious priest was brought in after being searched and cleared by security.

He requested the Pope to go with him to the far end of the chapel. He whispered his message to the Pope, knelt, kissed his ring and humbly said, "Let us all pay together to save us from those who want to harm us."

"Come my friends, let us all pray to the Lord to eradicate those who bring harm to Gods children." The Pope said and walked back to his two companions who sat dumbfounded at what has transpired before them.

They sat at the table, cupped their hands and shut their eyes.

The Pope began in a low voice, "O Lord, please accept from your humble servants, our request to get rid of those who mean harm to your people. Bring down your wrath of thunder and bolts of fire to show your anger to those who obstruct justice for the good of humanity. Give us those signs that will allow us to pray to do away with the new order to be imposed upon us to separate you from us, your children on this world. Amen."

The priest got up, kissed the ring on the Pope's hand, bowed to the other two and walked out.

"What did he tell you?" One of the religious representatives asked the Pope.

"Days of miracles have returned. That poor looking man of god had repeated apparitions some days ago, much before we planned to meet. An angle or whatever it was, foretold him of a force that will descend upon the Earth and try to change the order of things, and that we must pray to save our souls.

"He also narrated certain discussions that had taken place in the Vatican which only a few knew about, and also about your identities. How can a secluded priest in a remote village know all this? He must be someone special."

"You Holiness, he could be a spy to filter into our plans." The Muslim cleric said.

"Someone in the Vatican must be working with him." The Rabbi added.

"Nonsense, none in the Vatican can be so profane. Well, let us get down to what we have come for. That alien lady wants us to give up our traditions and set up a new world order. In due course she may ask us to give up our beliefs altogether. As innocent religious representatives of the faiths, we must approach her to reconsider her conditions on the restriction on religious travels outside our national borders." The Pope said.

"Remember what she said about the past, it is non-existent. Gone to ashes. We are reborn." The Rabbi pointed out with a big laugh.

"She can be nasty, and she may ask us, who are we to speak for all. Though we all worship one god, but which one. Each one of us have a different name for Him, and a different idea of what God is, so technically we do not worship the same All Mighty. Let us get our answers right before we make a fool of ourselves. How about asking the Hindus, Buddhists, Zoroastrians and some others to join in. A collective effort might distract her devious thinking." The Muslim cleric suggested.

"I think you have a point there. I will try to make contacts and will keep you posted. The Pope said, though in his mind he was uncomfortable.

Delighted with his achievement, the so called priest who is one of Ayond's informers, reported.

What he told her, "It is my suspicion that they plan to have an esoteric philosophical approach that may influence you to be more compassionate and lenient about your approach towards religions." He narrated verbatim the joint prayer they performed.

She was amused. "I must do what they want. To show His anger to those who want to obstruct for the good of humanity. Well, I shall oblige. In my opinion, they are the ones who want to hoodwink. Thunder and bolts of fire shall rain, as they have asked for it. Of course no bolts of fire but unprecedented harmless bolts of light in the shape of lightning. That should brighten their vision."

Ayond was in the mood for some innocuous fun to let those who preach goodness, but unknowingly sow the seeds of disorder.

Two days later Ayond with a few crew embarked on an excursion that would be amusing and at the same time will send a message to those concerned not to dabble in matters beyond their understandings, and just stick to their religious vows.

Ayond flew to Rome in one of her small crafts and parked above the city in its invisible form. It was a hot bright sunny Sunday afternoon. Cloud formation began to cover the metropolis, to their relief from the scorching sun, people became joyful. But not for long. Streaks of lightning display filled the canopy above accompanied by soft rumbling of thunder. Clouds became thicker obstructing the power of the sun. Fearing a heavy down pour, people quickly began to disperse.

All of a sudden, blinding lightning strikes stretching down touching the ground followed by deafening loud bursts of thunder that echoed throughout city. At the Vatican, the Pope looked out of a window and was in awe. A bolt of lightning grazed it and he jumped back, returned cautiously back, two more strikes and he decided to retire to another room and knelt in prayer. His first thought was that his message was misinterpreted. "I meant them, not us." He reminded.

An hour later, the clouds dissolved and the sun shone as if nothing had happened. People were amazed, with all what had happened, not a drop of rain or any damage from the bolts of lightning that struck buildings and pavements. They dismissed it as a miracle of God. "Perhaps some kind of warning," someone said.

Ayond moved to Jerusalem, and the same performance repeated. Next was to the city where the Islamic cleric lived.

Minutes later, all the three men of the faith were on the telephone, worried and distraught, they agreed to abandon their resolution.

"Let us agree not to meet and meddle with things beyond our control. God knows what is best for us and let the politicians do the rest, of course through His guidance." The Pope said.

Ayond returned with naughty grin on her face. "Sorry chaps, I just wanted to have some fun." She said to herself

CHAPTER 27

Days later, during a meeting in New York, working on the constitution for the New World Order, Ayond was alerted by Aishtra in London that Argos had received a message moon base that a number of Xanthumian ships were approaching Earth. She briefed Steve of the situation and excused herself to go and the meet the theat.

Within hours she returned to London and straight to the hanger. She left a few smaller vessels with Aishtra just in case a hostile situation arose. Ayond left on the mothership. Just beyond the moon detected the approaching Xanthumian ships. Being invisible, by passed them and began her approach from the rare. Several of her smaller vessels were released and circled the Xanthumian fleet.

On the screen of the Xanthumian lead ship Ayond's face appeared. To the surprise of the captain of the transgressor vessel, he uttered a loud insulting remark in his language. Promptly Ayond to retorted back with one filthy word that angered him.

He immediately threatened, "You human lover, cannot touch us, we have fleet that will destroy you and your fellow humans."

Ayond calmly warned, "Your entire fleet is surrounded."

"Can't see you or your fleet," He stopped. It suddenly dawned on him that they were invisible.

The Captain promptly fiddled with some instruments and Ayond's entourage of vessels came to his view, he could see them.

"You guessed right and I know you can see us now. I will demonstrate what I can do." A beam of light targeted one of his and blew it up.

Ayond gave another warning, "The same will happen to all of your vessels unless you surrender and bring all your ships' crew on to ours, I will allow you to return to your boss with a message, tell him soon he will feel our presence."

No response from the Xanthumian captain. Suddenly hell broke loose. The Xanthumian ships opened fire. Ayond's ship had its force shield up and with one command her smaller vessels came to action. They scrambled and with acrobatic maneuvers displayed their deadly weaponry. A fierce battle raged. During the ensuing skirmishes Ayond had placed her ship above the Xanthumian lead ship and began to draw it gently using magnetic force attraction and with a loud thump the two came into contact and was firmly in her grasp. The adversary realised what had happened, rendering it incapacitated. He cursed and swore. Ayond ignore him and assisted her fleet in zapping the enemy, soon all were eliminated.

The captain shouted, "For what you have done, Xanthum will destroy your planet and Earth too."

"Before that I will blow you to bits unless you shut up and surrender."

The captain tried to break away from her magnetic grip but to no avail. He released some of his smaller crafts to attack Ayond but they too were destroyed. Being under her ship, he was helpless, fearing he might cause damage to her ship she issued a warning. "If you continue to try to free yourself I will have no option but to destroy you."

"I will not surrender and being attached to your ship you are also a prisoner."

While dialogue between them was going on, the Xanthumian captain tried desperately to release his ship, to his disappointment the magnetic force was so strong that jammed some of its functions, smoke began to emerge from within the control panel and suddenly ignited and burst into flames.

Ayond had to make a decision.

"Captain this is my final warning, surrender and save yourself and your crew or face the consequences," Her voice was firm.

The Captain did not acknowledge and tried once more to disengage, Ayond had no choice but to detach his vessel with a repelling force that hurled the Xanthumian ship plummeting and struck it with a beam that shattered it instantaneously.

She sent a message to Urna and warned them of Xanthum, their leader's possible reprisal to attack their planet.

CHAPTER 28

Back on Earth Ayond with Steve and Justin continued working on the final touches of the New World Order. It had taken nearly a month to complete. The two week period she had committed at the United Nations to gather and get the members to join the new world order was delayed. That aroused more suspicion in the minds of some of the world leaders, perhaps more stringent rules were being contemplated.

Ayond invited all the leaders who had initially participated in their first meeting to her residence, the Facility in London. Each one was told confidentially where to meet to be picked up and transported to London by invisible small crafts. On arrival at the hanger in London, each was taken by Steve's security personnel to the Facility where they were accommodated.

By late afternoon attendants visited each guest and helped in dressing them up for the festive occasion that was to follow. A ceremonial hall was decked up for the occasion.

At the far end of the hall, on a podium an orchestra sat tuning their instruments. Sopranos, mezzo sopranos, Tenors, baritones and a few choir girls stood waiting for the VIPs' entrance.

On their arrival the lights dimmed and the music began to play Ode to Joy. An abridged version. When ended, amazed by the performance, they stood mesmerised for several second, then there were loud shouts of appreciation.

Ayond took the floor and welcomed her guests. "We would have loved to hear the whole symphony by Beethoven, but all the same, beside its melodious effects it also conveyed a message of joy, to bring people together, to live in harmony and courage.

"I am proud to say that all the players are from our planet and that is just a fraction of the good things we have learnt from you. I am thankful to all your Excellences to share this evening at our Facility which has been our home for many years. You will go down in history books to be the initiators of a better way of live, transforming this beautiful world into what it deserves to be, a Garden of Eden. Let us celebrate, let the party begin."

Soft music began and champagne bottles popped punctuating the noir ambiance. The atmosphere sobered when a dozen or more alien females dressed appropriately for the occasion joined in. To start a lead, David and the team picked partners and began to dance. The music flowed and the hours passed quickly. They were interrupted by the call for dinner. Later they retired to the lush lawn where brandy was served.

David overheard the Russian president saying to a counterpart, "Can't believe all this happing some hundreds of feet below the ground."

"If they can do all this here, I can trust them with what they can do above." The other said.

"Let us hope they will achieve that goal and make our home better." The Russian put in hopefully.

It was near midnight when they retired to their rooms.

The next morning, after having breakfast in their rooms, Ayond and Aishtra collected them and began the tour of the Facility.

They started with the library and the museum. "All these shelves were stacked with books, artefacts and documentary discs. Everything was transported to Urna when we left, there all is comfortably housed in a museum.

They got in a bus and were taken on a tour of a small shopping mall and to what was once a dairy farm. Ayond explained, "This was a thriving active place, now just a ghost town. There were hundreds of us living down here, now only essential personal. When we leave, we will hand over the keys to our trusted friend, Steve.

The last item on the agenda was to meet Argos.

They entered the chamber where Argos rested on a round table covered with golden foil. Ayond uncovered it and said something to it. Pinhead size lights began to glow, changing their colours to those of the rainbow. Then there was a gentle soft voice, "I welcome you to my humble abode, you can touch me to feel the warmth of your handshake." All lined up and touched him.

"I have a message from my master, the Supreme High which I will read out to you. It says and I quote, 'I thank you all for assisting Ayond in achieving what she has been sent to do. When I visit Earth, which will be soon, I will meet each one of you personally and extend my gratitude. In the meantime, keep smiling and the world will smile back. Have a safe journey back home, good bye."

Argos added, "He will see you when this transmission reaches him in about an hour."

The lights on Argos began to fade.

Few shouted, "Bye for now Argos."

Ayond led them to a fleet of cars waiting to take them to the hanger, from there they would be flown home.

As they left David commented to Sam, "After that tour and especially the meeting with Argos, a message is clearly conveyed about the alien's capabilities and sincere intentions."

"All those world leaders must have understood it loud and clear, but what about those who have not attended." Sam put in.

"Not all, but a few, even if they have seen what they have here, would still have an element of doubt. Too stubborn to change their ways." David observed.

"Too bad for them, they will be facing the music, with a loud crescendo." Sam added mischievously.

"I just hope it will not go on deaf years." David said with laugh.

CHAPTER 29

A week later, the Secretary General issued a two week deadline to join the New World Order. After that applicants must have valid reason for reconsidering. Within a week only fifty six nations applied and they announced the withdrawal of their ambassadors from non-members. Almost immediately thirty four opted to join. On the request of the nine executive members, a grace period of fourteen days was given. Seeing the seriousness of the situation, acceptance began to trickle in, bringing the total to one hundred and forty four.

Ayond was pleased, "We will go easy on those south and East Asian nations, they are still recouping from the trauma of the virus inflicted ten years ago. As far as the others who ignored our calling, sanction would apply."

Sanctions were to include the withdrawal of ambassadorial representation, stoppage of trading, road and air transport, and international telephone services. Within two weeks the effects were distressing. A few nations sent in their applications, conveying their apologies for not understanding the general concept of the new world order. The Secretary General replied with just one line. "Ignorance in all its forms is not a sufficient reason, your application is deeply regretted."

According to the set rules, they have to wait ten years for their membership to be considered. By then, even a rich nation would not be able to survive the economic shut down and will be reduced to a failed state.

Ayond reported her achievement to the Supreme High and he agreed to her return to Urna, "But before coming home, get rid of that evil Xanthum and his kind and turn Io where they live into a blazing moon." He also told her that the Guardian would be sent to head the New World Order, after spending some time with her to update him on Earth's current affairs.

Ayond broke the good news to the team and invited them to celebrate. At her residence they gathered, hosted a toast and she proudly declared, "The Earth is in good hands. The chosen five permanent and nine executive members have done well so far, and after the Guardian's arrival to take charge, we have nothing to worry about. Our bases on the moon will be vigilant, any disturbance will be met from there. Earth people will realize how quickly we can respond, they will think twice before causing any trouble."

"Cheers everyone!"

From distance someone asked, "When do we leave?"

"When Jupiter and its moons are at their closest point to Earth, and with our interstellar speed our journey back would take about five weeks max." Ayond said.

They had twelve days to spend, they decided to visit relatives and friends to say their goodbyes, perhaps for good.

One afternoon Fiona sat with Daniel alone in the garden. She looked stressed and burst into tears. "I have become part of you all and suddenly I am to be orphaned. I don't know how to get back to the world I left a few months ago. I feel that I do not belong to it anymore."

Daniel held her tight and tried to pacify her emotional outpouring. "We will miss you too. You have your parents and brother, soon you will adjust."

"It is true, as long as my parents are there I am comfortable, but when they are gone I will feel lonely. My brother has his own life and I don't think I will adjust after all this."

"There is one solution, why not come with us."

"I will be scared to live there alone."

"We will be there with you, you can get a job perhaps as a teacher, they love teachers and hold them in very high esteem. I will be there with you."

"Yes, but what about your religious work?"

"What religious work, it is not like here on Earth, there is no church or preaching as you know it. Life is different, no statues or any form of manmade structures to worship, it is all in the heart and the mind, each individual has his church within him or her."

She suddenly changed the subject, "How are the women there, are they like us?"

Physically yes, mentally superior, they are very graceful too, you will love their company."

"Do you have a friend there?"

"Many."

"What I meant, do you have a special close friend?"

"No, just what you might call, platonic."

"So if I am there I will be part of your platonic harem."

"Well," he paused for a moment, "In your case, my feeling for you is different, as a matter of fact, as I am talking to you, an inner feeling within me, which I cannot describe tells me that I am in love with you."

"You mean that?"

"Yes, I do. You must accompany us, we will be together, always."

"To be honest I always had a special feeling for you, I have loved you secretly."

"How wonderful, let's tell Ayond tomorrow, I am sure she will approve."

Ayond was glad to include Fiona and the news spread amongst the members of the team. There were jubilation and merry making till the early hours.

Fiona broke the news to her parents and a brief ceremony was performed.

"I am glad for you, enjoy life in a better world, perhaps someday your children or grandchildren will return home. I will ask your brother to share this house with them if and when they return, as a gift from their grandparents."

Sam, Daniel, Aishtra and David visited Michael, who had recouped to his normal health. He hugged Aishtra and made a request, "How about finding me a Jinn that I can marry and to keep me in good shape." They all laughed and said their good byes with tears in their eyes.

All returned to the Facility, it took them awhile to mentally recover and looked forward to their journey back to Urna.

The day of their departure arrived, the Prime Minister, Steve and Justin hugged each one of them. Bill held Fiona fondly and kissed her on the cheeks with tears in his eyes, "Will miss you, you have been a good secretary. You are in good hands, enjoy your new life."

The mother ship lifted off, they continued to wave until it became a speck and vanished from view.

CHAPTER 30

Few hours in the flight, Ayond left the controls to the co-pilot and joined the team for a cup of tea.

"I will miss tea, have taken sufficient stock to last me for some time and a lot of budding sprouts also, hope they survive the journey. I will be the only one to have a tea garden on Urna," Ayond continued, "Now let me tell you our schedule before we reach home. I have an unfinished business to settle with Xanthum. You all shall witness what happens to creatures who misbehave. He had been warned several times but keeps pestering the neighbourhood, whenever he gets a chance. The evil traits embedded in him would never vanish, and the best thing to do is to eliminate him and his kind once for all and make the solar system free from their constant threats.

"Once I hand over charge to the Guardian, Earth will no longer be my responsibility. I will have plenty of time to nurse my garden with a lot of fruits, vegetables and flowers, of course not forgetting my prime crop, *tea.*"

During the flight, the living conditions were like being in a housing complex. It does not give the claustrophobic environment of smaller vessels. Sporting facility, movie-theater, library, café and a pub. All, including the staff live as one big happy family.

The journey was long but time moved quickly with the joyful environment within. Weeks passed. When they were in the vicinity of Urna, Ayond contacted the Supreme High. She sought his final approval to continue her journey to Jupiter's moon Io, where the Xanthumians reside and to eliminate them; to which he agreed.

Just before reaching Jupiter, the ship decelerated. Io was about a few hours journey from there. Ayond's ship was spotted by the adversary's security fleet orbiting Io. They informed Xanthum, their leader. He wasted no time, got into his vessel, accompanied by small torpedo like crafts. Ayond acted fast, she also released a few small tactical crafts. To cause a distraction to the oncoming adversary war machines, they opened fire and were engaged in combat. While that was happening, Ayond turned her ship invisible. She saw Xanthum on the screen, and he could see her, but could not see her ship. She was amused by his panicking gestures.

While in that situation, Ayond placed her ship above his and began to draw it gently by using the magnetic force field. When the two metallic hulls met and there was a loud thud, only then Xanthum realised that his vessel was in the grip of some force that caused its immobility, by a power he could not see. He was furious.

He ordered some of his torpedo crafts to investigate, but failed to see any source. Ayond took the opportunity to annihilate them as they were easy targets. As a precaution she put up the ship's force field. Xanthum tried to get visuals on the outside and picked the invisible fire power coming from above his ship that was routing his defences. He guessed that her ship was invisible. Ayond's face appeared on his screen, mockingly she said, "Your turn is coming soon, but first I want you to enjoy watching the extermination of your entire fleet."

He hissed and threatened to blow her ship.

"I have just neutralised the functions on your ship, now you are my prisoner." She said calmly.

Xanthum played with the controls, they were non-functional. He shouted at his crew to do something, but to no avail.

"Just sit and watch," She said, but to her disappointment the adversary's torpedo like crafts were having the upper hand battling her smaller crafts, and her fleet seemed to be losing.

"You better release me and I will spare your lives, soon they will come for you." Xanthum said proudly, hissed and grunted.

Ayond released some more of her small crafts and the battle continued. Xanthum knew that in the present state he had no chance to win. Surreptitiously he left the cabin. Once out, he ran through corridors and entered a room, slipping through a tube which landed him into a bay where there was an escape shuttle in case of an emergency. He sat in it and tried to activate it, but it failed to start. He realised that Ayond had paralysed all the functions on his ship and whatever is on it. He got out of the shuttle and tried to open the panel hatch manually, to slip out into space, but that too failed. He cursed and tried again and again. He was trapped, and could not get back to the top.

Meanwhile, not knowing his fate, Ayond busied herself in aiding her fleet to get rid of the enemy torpedo like crafts. They were all eradicated and she breathed a sigh of relief. Not seeing Xanthum on the screen she suspected that he was up to something that might harm her ship, and decided to act. Without warning she disengaged his ship from the magnetic grip and with a repellant force sent it tumbling, zapped it with one deadly strike, disintegrating it to tiny fragments.

"That is the end of Xanthum, now to eliminate the rest of his kind, once and for all. She ordered what was left of her fleet to assemble behind her. Flew low and approached Io. They descended close to the surface and began their onslaught, torched it as they encircled the moon in continuous successions until it turned into a flaming sphere.

"That is the end of that menace, Xanthum and his evil lot. There will be no trace of them having ever existed. Should have done it long ago. Now to head back home to Urna." Ayond said and joined her colleagues and asked for a strong cup of tea.

"I see tea has become a fashion with you, you will have to train some women to do the plucking as it needs delicate hands." David said.

"Who says so, we can change that. As you guys will have very little to do from now on, will get you trained how to pluck. You will enjoy the brew better after a hard day's work." Ayond said playfully.

Before reaching Urna, her last act as the captain was to summon Fiona and Daniel. Both were unaware of what was to come. Both stood in front of her, "You wanted us?" Daniel asked.

"Yes my good friends, I know exactly what is in your minds, so let us get it done. I want to do this as the last act of my command on this ship. Who knows when I shall have such privilege again? To make two people happy is like conquering the world. Daniel and Fiona, to make me happy, please hold hands." Fiona was thrilled as she guessed her intentions.

Ayond solemnly said, "Fiona will you take Daniel as your loving husband."

"Yes," Fiona replied.

"Daniel, will you take Fiona as your beloved wife."

His answer came, "Yes, I do."

"As the captain of the ship, by the authority invested in me, I pronounce you man and wife." She was brief. The team looked on and all said with one voice, "Let's kiss the bride."

It was not tea, but champagne bottles popped and they all danced.

Back on Urna, the Supreme High was delighted by Ayond's achievements and the demise of their adversary going back thousands of years, freeing the solar system from an evil resident. He then requested not to be disturbed until such time he wished to meet them. His last words were, "Enjoy yourselves, you all deserve it. Meanwhile, I shall do what is to be done."

Ayond tried for long to read between the lines what the Supreme High meant by his last words. "It is perhaps nothing," She gave up.

At her home on Urna, Ayond invited the team and some friends to celebrate their home coming. Sometime during the party she whispered to David, "I am already missing Earth."

CHAPTER 31

Several weeks later, Ayond and her Earth colleagues prepared to celebrate, once in three years phenomena on Urna that lasts for three days, known as 'Argoshtak'. They met an hour before dawn, spread their rugs on the neatly manicured patch of grass just below Ayond open terrace, "I have brought some cushions and some covers just in case it gets chilly. As we have a few minutes before it starts, let me explain what this wonder is about." Ayond began, "This marvel which we call Argoshtak happens every three years and lasts for three days. We have no idea what it is and where it comes from. It just materialises out of nowhere, its schedule is fixed by the hours and minutes. We can predict its appearance for many years to come. Our scientists failed to find an answer, so we just treat it as a spectacle to be enjoyed. For some reason, it helps the growth of trees, grass and better crops yields. We begin to feel a kind of zest to do more. It is like refreshing nature for better days to come. It is certainly a miracle of some kind.

"You all have been on Urna for ten years but unfortunately during the period of Argoshtak occurrences we either have been on space missions surveying planets, moons, or on visits to Earth. Lucky for all of us to have returned just in time for you to witness this happy occasion.

"Shortly you will see its enigmatic entrance. A thousand feet or so above a haze of white fog-like vapour begins to envelope the entire planet, gradually changing into strips of rainbow colours, starts to move westwards and encircles the planet in a continuous motion. After a while an extraordinary transformation takes place, in the middle of the strips, a large oval shaped form begins to take shape like a buckle in a belt, filled with cloudy cumulous formations churning gently with concentrated deep purple flashing lights. Once it completes a circle, the entire system gently revolves and settles down for a short while. Then it starts all over again and the process carries on. This continues for three days and finally ends with all the colours merging and fading away. Now you know what to expect. You all may hear some of our people in joyous moods." She paused and before she could begin again, Jim interrupted.

"You mean to say this has been a permanent feature all those years and no with change?"

"A good question, from our records, many thousands of years ago, the display was of a different nature before this miraculous change. It was just red with black mix and when it appeared people became lethargic and sick. A phenomena of electromagnetic forces or some mysterious solar chemicals, we still do not know what it was."

Sam was listening attentively and broke in, "Your technology has failed to analyze this marvels, and it must be very special. There has to be an answer."

Daniel raised his hand and said thoughtfully, "Ayond you said, many years ago the colours were different and made people unhappy but later changed to what we are seeing today that it makes you happy and refreshed. Could be the reason for the transformation by someone or something that was unhappy at one time and after seeing a good change became pleased and hence this gift."

"There are many hypothesis, well let us not trouble our heads, just enjoy the day," Ayond said softly, not wanting to get into what Daniel was driving at.

"To change the subject," Fiona butted in, "I am quite fascinated by how you restructured Urna after your long journey sailing in space as a rouge planet and its miraculous inclusion in our solar system. It must had suffered badly, but from what I see can't imagine it ever happened. You have done wonders by transforming it to what it is today. Through your technological applications, harnessed the heat from the sun making it as good as any place on Earth."

"Hard work and a lot of help from the Supreme High. His technological guidance made it possible. We put up many satellites to harness the sun's poor light to make it warm and shiny. After that the rest was easy. Vegetation, trees and insects began to multiply and here we are sitting in the open with trees around us and birds flying above. All of them were brought from Earth, along with cats, dogs, deer and several other species.

"Every three years a cycle of progress starts for the better. You will be here to see more changes," Ayond concluded.

"What a dream world this place is, thank you for letting us share it with you," Fiona was appreciative.

Soon the sky above began to be enveloped by a white fog-like mist. An hour later, faint streaks of the rainbow were taking shape, a little later the entire canopy above was like a fairy tale world, adding to the spectacle, it started to rotate.

The sun rose and brightened the colours, for hours they watched and in between hot tea warmed the chilly morning air. Sometime later they went in for breakfast and returned to continue their watch. By then the miraculous change above displayed the buckle shaped whirling of concentrated thick purplish gelatinous substance with lightning discharges.

Ayond came over to find David reclining reading a book. "Don't be a bore,' she said, snatched the book, lay down beside him giving him a hug."

David reciprocated and both stretched themselves and stared at the wonder up.

By midday all dispersed and decided to meet again on the third day, to witness the fading of Argoshtak.

Ayond planned a befitting send off to the natural enigma. Dinner and dance to welcome another phase of prosperity.

On the third day they arrived an hour before the finale of nature's mysterious exhibit.

"Soon this beautiful skyscape will disappear, nobody knows where it comes from or goes to," Ayond said softly.

"Whatever it is, I have enjoyed every minute of it." David put in ethically.

Ayond spotted Daniel and Fiona in an embrace, "They are so well adjusted here, and loved by everyone. I am thinking of establishing a school where people with special gifts of knowledge and mental power can cultivate their abilities and make Daniel in charge with Fiona to assist him."

The setting sun turned golden and the colours above began to fade into nothingness.

They collected all the paraphernalia that lay scattered on the grass and moved in to Ayond's residence.

"A toast for the coming season. May it brings prosperity as always," Ayond raised her glass and all rushed and clicked hers and with one voice they shouted, "Cheers."

The party went on, some moved out to the terrace, others sat chatting in the living room. In a corner Aishtra and Fiona sat alone.

"Tell me Aishtra, I never had a chance to sit with you and talk freely. How did you all meet and became a tied knit. I read the formal report of how you all got together finding the Medallion etc. etc. but I want to know more about each person, after all we are a family now."

Aishtra thought for a moment and let out a sigh, "It is a long story but I will be brief. Sam, my husband has two cousins, Daniel your husband and Michael who is on Earth. Sam is a civil contractor and Daniel ran a church, well you know all about that. Jim, who is Sam's friend ran an antique shop and is well versed with ancient languages and artifacts. He has two sons who decided to stay behind and take their chances on the troubled Earth. His wife decided to join him on Urna and both are happily settled. She is sitting at the far end with Jim. I will introduce you to her.

"As far as David is concerned, he had lost his wife much earlier and had two son. Unfortunately both were killed in one of the terrorist attacks. I suspect that he has a soft corner for Ayond.

"To conclude, we are one happy family and you made a wise decision to move to Urna."

"What about you, tell me more of your kind? You said you are made of smokeless fire, it makes no sense," Fiona asked.

"On Earth this expression is used simply to say we are specially made from fire. But actually we are made from what you term as electromagnetic impulses. Hence we have special capabilities such as to change our shape, travel with almost the speed of light and have higher faculty of brain power."

"They say you are from Earth, but how are you different, all the Earth people are human like me," Before Fiona could finish her sentence Aishtra cut in.

"I am coming to that. The Earth is four and half billion years old. The first two or so billion years was in its formation stage and as it cooled methane and carbohydrates were the primary products and electromagnetic activity just as you have today on Saturn's moon Titan, with pools of those gasses. A billion years or so later a life form began to emerge. That life form was the beginning of our species, and by the way, the carbohydrates and methane developed into what is known today as crude oil. As time went by we began to populate the planet. Many million years later the planet's geology and its oceans, played in the emergence of oxygen and other gases replacing the atmospheric and ecological structure; another form of life began to evolve. The humans evolved. They flourished and soon developed arsenals and reduced themselves to the stone-age. That was the human specie's first emergence. It took many many years to reappear for the second time. We knew that they will again reach a stage to do away with each other. At one time the King of the Jinn decided to exterminate them, but his advisors intervened to let them be, time will tell if they will be better than their predecessors. The rest is history."

Fiona listened attentively and put a question to Aishtra. "When humans emerged the second time, why you did not make an effort to introduce yourselves and exchange your knowledge and technology, after all you had a head start and could have lived happily together. Humans would have been different today."

"A good question. We as Jinn, have understood the meaning of life, having the capability to travel in space, settled on moons in the solar system made new homes and lived with entities not yet known to you humans, in a way we have become masters of all we surveyed. But with their emergence the second time, humans were no different from their predecessors. Aggression is in their blood. Acts of killing one another is a common feature of survival for food, tools and territory. We knew that someday they would compete with us and bring violence to our door steps and disturb our peace. So we ignored them, though there was a time when besides trying to destroy them, we contemplated on manipulating their genetic system. One more thing, many Jinn men and women have fallen in love with humans and their children and grandchildren have brought about the technological skills such as inventors, scientist and mathematicians and so on. That is all I have to say, and as far as you and I living on this heavenly Urna, we have nothing to worry about."

Fiona got up and hugged Aishtra. While still in an embrace, they heard Ayond voice in the distance, "Hear me everyone, please excuse me, I have to leave you all. Continue until I return." A ring that she always wore, is a device to alert her of any incoming messages.

She walked through a narrow corridor and stopped at a door. She whispered a word, there was a click, the door slid open and as she entered the lights came on automatically. A screen on a desk came to life. It flickered for a moment and settled with a light blue colour.

Ayond became attentive, she knew that colour meant that the Guardian wanted to speak to her. They talked very briefly in their language. Ayond remained fixed to the blank screen thinking. "The Supreme High wants to meet me and my Earth colleagues, why this request all of a sudden."

She got up and went back to the living room where she was greeted with pin drop silence. "What has happened in here, why the sad faces," Ayond asked in a loud voice.

David stood and walked up her. "The way you left the room, we felt you were under stress. I hope all is okay with you?"

"Of course I am alright. I have a special request from the Supreme High, he wants to meet us tomorrow at his chamber. He didn't say why. We will meet at the main administrative building at noon. Meanwhile, continue with what you are doing, have fun, tomorrow is another day."

They all gathered and exchanged guesses as to why the highest authority on the plant wants to see them. "Perhaps he wants to send us back to Earth for another assignment," Sam put in softly.

"But we have just come back, it makes no sense," Jim said.

"No need to make guesses, we'll find out tomorrow. Let's sleep on it," David said.

The next day at the appointed time they were received by Ayond at the main administrative building. Two attendants escorted them to a room adjacent to the Supreme High's chamber. Shortly after, the Guardian entered.

"Pleasure to meet you all again," He said and turned to Ayond, "How about introducing me to our latest members," Walked up to Fiona and extended his hand. To Fiona he looked very much human, "To me he is a normal being, though much taller, not an android as they had given me that impression, good-looking too." She thought.

Then he turned to Saeed, "I want to thank you for what you have done to assist us in procuring that device, I am sure you are well and happily settled."

"It was a pleasure to assist, it was my duty to return that piece to the rightful owners," Saeed put in softly.

To Jim's wife he said, "I am glad you made up your mind to join your husband. Hope he is behaving himself?"

"Thank you Mr. Guardian, I could not be happier, Jim is behaving nicely."

When all the formalities were completed he requested them to follow him. They entered a larger room and Guardian said, "I welcome you to the chamber of the Supreme High."

The chamber had two sections divided by a golden curtain. In the front was a row of chairs facing a large screen on the wall. Behind them, the golden curtain separated them from the room where the Supreme High resided. They sat and waited. The Guardian walked up and faced them. "The Supreme High has some deliberations to make. We will hear his voice only and as he speaks you will see images projected from his memory on to the screen. He will explain what those represent. Kindly be attentive." The lights dimmed.

After a few moments, the voice of the Supreme High came through speakers.

"Thank you all for coming. Ayond, you have three new members added to your Earth team, the Egyptian Saeed, Fiona and Jim's wife. I welcome them too," After a brief pause he continued, "I am feeling very happy today and want to share with you some of my memories that go back many thousands of years. Some are recorded in our archives which you and Aishtra must have read. Today I will project some of those memories in visual form. I have invited your team to share this happy occasion. After I finish, the Guardian has a surprise for you."

Ayond wondered what the surprise would be. Her enquiring mind was active.

The Supreme High's voice continued, "Please watch with no interruptions. Make notes, after the show the Guardian or I will answer your questions. I will begin with scenes from the planet where I was made, starting from the time I came to life.

The screen showed landscapes of evergreen fields, moving further the scene changed to a thick forest with cascading waterfalls, birds flying aimlessly against a blue sky and animals drinking from a steam that meandered into the distance.

Then the view shifted to a bustling city with tall buildings and tiny vehicles flying about. Streets buzzing with life.

"Those people were human-like in many ways, made of flesh and blood. They were energetic and hardworking, and had reached the zenith of a mature race. To give you some idea of their capabilities, they had mastered space travel when people on Earth were in the process of evolving into Homo sapiens. Sadly, all of a sudden, out of nowhere calamity struck. Nature played havoc on the entire planet, a freak storm lashed mercilessly followed by several days of rain that had a greenish tinge. Its effect showed up months later when some trees, not all, began to wither and die. The strange thing was that some plant life survived and had no apparent effect on animals and people.

"Sometime later it was noticed that the birthrate in all living begins was dwindling, something was causing sterility. Analysis showed water was the cause. That mysterious rainfall had changed its biological structure. To compensate for the falling manpower, they introduced robots to do menial and factory jobs. In this scene you can see all the factory workers are robots.

"As the population was getting older and young generation declining, more intelligent robots were made to fill in the shortage in offices and androids to assist the senior management. Subsequently more highly advance androids were developed to run the affairs of the community. A time came when another intelligent machine was needed to help in directing the affairs of the planet and have control on the artificial intelligence entities, such as robots and androids. That machine was invented, more sophisticated than they could have imagined. It also had the capability to control the weather and attach itself to the electromagnetic field of the planet. It was the ultimate form of entity that one can think of. It could speak and give commands. They called it the master machine."

Scenes on the screen showed robots, androids and people being directed by that machine. Looking at the master machine, Ayond exchanged glances with some next to her, "That looks like our Supreme High." She thought

The voice continued, "As time went by, life form reached a critical level, soon all life would be extinct. On the master machine's suggestion, they created highly intelligent advanced androids that would assist the master machine to supervise and run the day to day functions of the administration. Their bodily appearance was human, though a bit taller. We manipulated their pineal glands and introduced new features to the brain to enable them to change their physical self into photons.

"To administer that function, on the screen you see a handsome male form, with a slight sheen to the skin and shiny cranium. With its 'will power' so to speak, he can change his form into photons or light waves. Watch carefully how it will beam itself as a ray of light." An aura of faint bluish light began to radiate around its form which became intense until it turned into a splotch. Within an instant it shot out through the window and appeared on the outside. "With this ability it can travel in space as a wave length of light for millions of miles."

Ayond looked at the Guardian who sat at the far end. "If I am not wrong, that must have been the Guardian or one of his kind." She thought.

"As time went by, living beings became very sparse, they knew that very soon there would be none left. They made a decision to build a refuge to house the master machine where it will reside and function. They collected all the humanlike androids and decided to name them as the 'keepers' of the planet under the command of the master machine.

"Now you see the entire planet gone dead, no living begins, some trees and polluted streams. All life forms perished, leaving the planet with robots and older forms of androids. The master machine instructed the keepers to dismantle the lower forms of robots and androids as there was no more use of them. The only inhabitants or *living presence* on the planet were the master machine and the keepers.

"The master machine called all the keepers and said to them that there was no need to stay on this dying planet, *'go out into space and seek out new worlds that have life and help them to promote their wellbeing, and those who have already achieved higher order, further their knowledge.'* The master machine then asked them to put him on sleep mode and secure the entrance of his habitat with a code that only they can operate."

A bird eye view of the planet showed deserted landscapes that had changed over a long period of time into a barren desert and decayed fallen structures that hinted at a civilisation that had once thrived.

The voice continued, "It was pathetic, but life in worlds come and go, even planets, have a time scale, when their time is up they are swallowed by their star or disintegrate into a cataclysmic accident.

"Coming back to the keepers, one happened to land on your planet Urna,"

The words, keepers and Urna, triggered an impulse on all who were watching, they turned to the Guardian's chair. It was empty, he had left the room.

There was a pause on the screen and the voice said in a low tone, "He left the room not to be embarrassed. He will join you later."

The screen came to life again.

"When the keeper had first visited your planet Urna, many thousands of years ago, he landed in the southern part which was thickly forested and inhabited by fierce savages. A fierce battle with axes and spears raged with bodies strewn all over, some dead and dying. His sudden appearance in the midst of it as a beam of light made the waring warriors freeze and were horrified by his apparition. I remember him projecting his thoughts into my mind when he narrated the incident sometime later. It was humorous the way he described the scene, though pitiful. However, in their midst his form began to change to a brassy figure, and to add to the enigma, the sun's reflection dazzled his form. He stood motionless for some time.

"The stunned warring tribes, after some deliberations among themselves, most fell to ground and lay flat on their faces in reverence, while some in warlike actions threw spears and axes uttering loud verbal grunts and snorts. The figure watching the scene unfolding in front of him, just raised one hand and said softly in his language, 'I am sorry to have disturbed your little game. Where am I?'"

"There was no reaction, but someone was brave enough to approach him and throw a spear which bounced off his leg and fell harmlessly to the ground. The figure was not amused but sent a harmless powerful beam of light. Seeing it coming out of his eyes, they prostrated and fell to the ground.

"Soon after, all the warring parties crawled towards him and stood up, formed a circle. Someone stepped out and with a gentle gesture pointed to the trees and started to walk toward them. The keeper walked in the middle of that procession, his figure stood tall, compared to their five feet average height. They entered the forest, fought their way through branches and unruly bushes, finally settled in a circular open area with a canopy of high trees and branches that surrounded them obstructing the sunlight from reaching the ground. They led him to a vertical rock formation and made him sit below it. With ceremonial vocal chants they bowed and prostrated. To them he was a god.

"He wanted to tell them the contrary but had no means to do so. A language barrier. That night he spent sitting alone under the towering rock while the entire tribe settled for the night. A thought struck him to leave the planet, but he remembered the master machine's instructions, *'go out into space and seek out worlds that have life and help them in promoting their life style.'* Another idea came to his mind, to explore the planet and learn more about it."

The scene changed with the keeper hopping from spot to spot across a massive island continent surrounded by a large ocean. To his delight he came across a very large stretch in the northern part of the continent, with flickering lights indicating the presence of active life in a cosmopolitan city with high rise building that stretched endlessly in all directions and flying vehicles darting to and fro.

The voice continued with a bit of humour, "Lost in bewilderment he did not realise that he was being watched. A flying vehicle hovered above where he stood. It landed besides him, a human form emerged and came up to him. Curiously studied him from head to toe.

"Where does he come from, his dress is strange and yet he looks more or less like me," the person thought.

The keeper picked his thoughts, facial expressions and hand movements and guessed what he was trying to convey.

In the same way he communicated back. The stranger understood partially that he comes from far away and wants to meet persons of wisdom and faculties of science. He then took him to a place where the keeper was welcomed. In a short time they taught him the language and all about their way of life. Later he was introduced to the council of administrators who governed the community. There were three, who had the final word, they were scientists. To them the keeper was far above their standard in knowledge and the sciences, he was elevated to the council of administrators.

"The keeper was fascinated by their space travels and visited their binary system which had seven planets. Only theirs had life with perpetual sun light. Only on the Polar Regions, the sun dimed for a short time.

"The keeper remembered the people he had met when he had first landed and decided to visit them. He arrived late night and sat at the rock and waited for them. In the morning a few appeared from their forest habitat and on seeing him they called loudly announcing his return. They assembled around him and fell in prostration and began to chant, 'Our god has come back.' They crawled up to him and kissed his feet.

"The keeper stood up and waved his hand and asked them to stay away, spoke in their language which he had recently learnt. In a calm comforting voice, 'I am not a god, but a person you can learn from, I can teach you healing powers and to prevent diseases, do away with killing each other and make you grow better food.'

"Someone asked him, who is his father? To which he replied that he has no father and no sons, he is all alone and eternal. In a short while he thought them to do away with superstation and ignorance, only then they can be better people. His sojourns to visit them were often, not to the knowledge of the northern people.

"The keeper thought of the master machine and arranged an expedition to visit his former planet. Arriving there was not a welcomed sight. Barren and lifeless, buildings reduced to rubble. The only standing structure was that which housed the master machine. The keeper knew the code to enter that solitary abode.

"The keeper flew to the top of the tower and held the pointed rod protruding from it, pressed hard and it jumped, he pulled it a few feet up and there was a loud click. Went down and touched a section of the wall, put both palms of his hand against it and uttered a few illegible words. There was a faint sound of a click, he uttered a word and spelt the letters. A panel began to slide open. They entered, the scene inside was uninviting, dull and claustrophobic. They peeled off the covering on it and carefully removed the machine.

"Back at Urna the master machine was housed in a special section in the council building. Only the council members and the keeper were allowed to interact with it. The Council decided to name the keeper, Guardian, as he had contributed wealth of knowledge to the welfare of the planet.

For a long time life on Urna was thriving with the guidance of the master machine, then most unexpectedly and for some unknown reason the planet began to wobble as if the gravitational attraction of the binary systems were having a tug of war. One of the suns had a greater pull and with that tug it lost its gravitational hold of the planet and hurled it into space. Luckily it just drifted away smoothly without much loss of life, luckily the atmosphere held on by its gravity. To make it easy for you to picture our predicament, do you remember a fiction serial shown by the BBC on television in the 70s called 'Space: 1999 when Earth's moon drifted away due to an accident. It was just like that what we had experienced. The master machine managed to stabilize the magnetic field distortions and sailed smoothly through the void of space. For many years we drifted into the unknown and by sheer luck entered the Earth solar system."

Sam was the only one who had seen those series and knew exactly how they must have felt. Now he was watching something not unfamiliar to him. The others just watched in suspense.

The scene on the screen showed the Guardian herding people on to space ships and their landing on Earth near the confluence of five rivers in what is today Pakistan. Rich evergreen land.

"None of us knew the fate of our world. But luckily it got caught by the sun and was placed in the solar system."

The scene changed to some getting into the ships and landing between the Tigress and Euphrates in Iraq. Further explorations led them to the Nile basin. "In the scenes here, you can see the work on the Sphinx, the pyramids in Egypt and Central America. The locals who were used as labour, thought us to be gods and there was a time they began to worship us.

"A general view shows what the world looked like. These images are from the memory of the Guardian who was actively involved.

"As a final note, that master machine we talked about earlier, was me and I am still here. Not forgetting the Guardian role, without him the fate of Urna would have been different. I was a stationary object giving instructions and the Guardian implemented them.

"Perhaps there will be many occasions in the future when we can recap more memories. For now I must say goodbye and my final meeting with you in my present state."

Ayond again pondered over the Supreme High's words, 'my final meeting and present state'. She was uncomfortable.

They were interrupted by the Guardian's cheerful appearance.

"Hello everyone, from today's talk you have come to know my true age, and of course the Supreme High's. It is a great wonder how we came to be. We were made by people like you, but have superseded them. They have implanted in our so called brain, a certain function, it was experimental but has successfully worked, which enables it to keep maturing in wisdom, keeps developing indefinitely, self-generating if you may. How it works we have no idea. Only time will tell to what extent.

"We shall be in debt to those who made us. They shall be in our memory for as long as we are functional. As a worn out part in us can be replaced, we can teach humans how to replace some parts of their body to enable them to live longer.

"The remark the Supreme High had made, got Ayond and perhaps all of you, curious, will be explained in due course."

The Guardian requested them to stand and face the golden curtain. They knew the Supreme High in his cube-form always resided there. The lights where they stood gradually died out. They were in complete darkness. The golden curtain began to slide gently, a strong pin light from the centre of the ceiling fell on a shadowy form sitting motionless on a chair on a dais. The onlookers wondered who or what is that form.

More lights came on. They could clearly see a man. The Guardian walked up to the dais, and faced the bewildered audience. Proudly he announced, "Ladies and gentlemen, I am delighted to introduce to you the Supreme High, in person."

They all gasped. The figure stood up. They could see a handsome man in his forties with a charming permanent smile, his skin colour light brown with a tinge of gilded shine and a bare cranium.

The Guardian continued, "It took me and a few others to change him from a stationery cube into a physical form like me, to enjoy the freedom of mobility and the outside world. He also has the function of beaming like a ray of light, like me. Could not think of another appearance, my form was the ultimate choice, though made him a few inched taller with a gilded shine, different from my brassy or metallic."

Shortly after, he descended from the pedestal and walked towards his dumbfounded audience accompanied by the Guardian. The Supreme High extended his hands to Ayond and hugged her. "I have always wanted to do this, you have been a good inspiration in my work." He turned to Aishtra, "You too, I am happy you found the right man. Sam is responsible for what we have achieve." He greeted each member of the team individually, to Fiona he said, "You and Aishtra looked fabulous in your displays in the holograms, but you both look much better in person. I am very happy to be *alive,* in the true sense of the word. Thanks to the Guardian who worked so hard to re-invent me.

He met each of Ayond's Earth colleagues, shook their hands and conversed.

"I have decided to let Ayond run the affairs of Urna while I take a short trip to Earth and enjoy the beauty of its gifts which its occupants have not yet discovered. The Guardian will take up his new post as the head of the New World Order until such time a human will qualify. But before I leave," He turned to Ayond," How about showing me some of that tea you keep boasting about." They all laughed and shortly afterwards they assembled at Ayond's home, sat on the open terrace sipping the brew.

At one corner Ayond and the Supreme High sat, while she kept sipping her hot tea, he just looked on. "Stop staring at me, do some justice to what you have in front of you." Ayond reprimanded the Supreme High.

He looked down at the plate in which tea shoots lay.

"It is sad that I cannot have that pleasure to drink that brew as I am a machine but still can appreciate what it offers, using my senses."

He picked a stem and brought it to his nose, moved it forward and back several times and there was a gentle sound like a deep breath of gratification. He put a few leaves in his mouth and chewed. After a long minute, he removed the gnawed foliage and said, "That is the best thing happened to me since I have become alive."

That is the end of a beautiful adventure.

Special thanks to:

Rasheda Kabir

I appreciate your proof reading help.